Sten Eirik
Géline of Acadie

Géline
of Acadie

Based on the poem
Evangeline by H.W. Longfellow

Sten Eirik

NIMBUS
PUBLISHING

Nimbus Publishing Limited
P.O. Box 9301, Station A
Halifax, NS B3K 5N5
(902) 455-4286

Design Editor: Kathy Kaulbach
Project Editor: Alexa Thompson
Cover and text illustrations: Gilles Archambault

Printed and bound in Canada

Canadian Cataloguing in Publication Data

Eirik, Sten.

Géline of Acadie
(NewWaves)
Based on the poem Evangeline by H.W. Longfellow.
ISBN 1-55109-021-X

I. Archambault, Gilles.   II.Longfellow, Henry Wadsworth, 1807-1882. Evangeline. III. Title. IV. Series.

PS8559.I74G45 1993   jC813'.54C93-098580-X
PZ7.E57Ge 1993

To
Jude, Joel, Andrea
and my parents Eva and Fred
and to the memory of my grandfather
Eirik Hornborg

Acknowledgements

For facilitating my research and growing acquaintance
with Acadian history, I owe thanks to:
Maurice Tugwell and the Acadia University Research
  Institute
Henri Paratte
Barbara LeBlanc
Sally Ross
the Nova Scotia Department of Tourism & Culture

For examining and nuturing my work as a critic and a
friend, I wish to thank:
Mary Wentz
Kimberley Smith
Alexandra Thompson
and, of course, Dorothy Blythe, who shared the sense
of this story from day one.

My other acknowledgement is to Henry Wadsworth
Longfellow, whose words and phrases I have
occasionally adopted.

—The Author

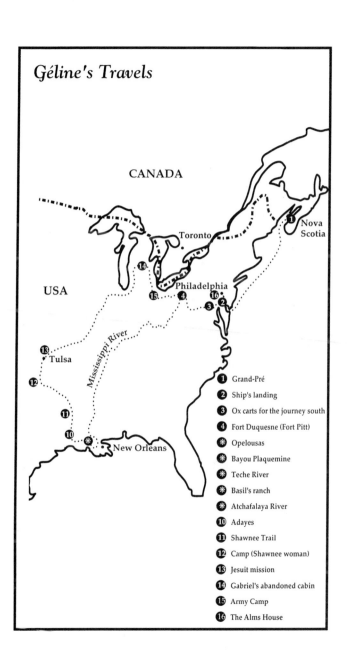

Géline's Travels

CANADA

Toronto

Nova Scotia

USA

Philadelphia

Mississippi River

Tulsa

New Orleans

1 Grand-Pré
2 Ship's landing
3 Ox carts for the journey south
4 Fort Duquesne (Fort Pitt)
❋ Opelousas
❋ Bayou Plaquemine
❋ Teche River
❋ Basil's ranch
❋ Atchafalaya River
10 Adayes
11 Shawnee Trail
12 Camp (Shawnee woman)
13 Jesuit mission
14 Gabriel's abandoned cabin
15 Army Camp
16 The Alms House

1

SHE HELD HER BREATH. But all she could hear was her heart pounding. She tried to stop its beating, just for an instant. If only the sun would hurry up and set, she thought. It would be out of her eyes. Squinting fiercely, she peered toward the crest of the hill. There was a quiver in the tall grass, yes, but was it Alphonse or just the wind? She was on her own. Emilie and Baptiste had crawled through the bramble patch to the far side of the clearing. They might be getting ready to attack. But Géline knew she had no choice. To get close enough, she would have to run those thirty feet in the open and dive for cover behind the old, uprooted clods of the dead cedar.

There it was again, a sudden ripple where the grass touched the sky. But was it Alphonse and Gabriel? Or had they left the fort to set up an ambush already? She peered anxiously up and down the hillside. There was no hint of danger. The air hummed with bees, and butterflies flitted from straw to straw. Clouds were slumbering far over the Basin, touched with gentle gold. A bead of sweat rolled from her hair into her left eyebrow. She had to risk it.

Taking a firm hold of the gun, she inched her way up onto her feet. Still no fire from the hill. With a surge of glorious bravery, she lunged across the grass and made for the safety of the fallen cedar. *Alphonse, that creep!* Didn't she see his pale, bony face rising gleefully on the hill! Then came the dread sound of gunfire.

"P'choo! P'choo-p'choo-p'choo!"

She snaked her way from side to side, dodging the speeding bullets.

"You're dead, Géline!" That was Alphonse, demanding fair play.

"But I ducked!" shouted Géline and flung herself recklessly behind the cedar. Her head was pounding and her knees shaking, as she awaited the inevitable.

"You can't duck a bullet, you goose. Why do we have to have girls, Gabriel? They ruin everything." His voice was high and whining now. "Do you hear, either you count fifty or I'm not playing any more!"

Géline knew that Alphonse would have no compunction about walking out on the adventure they had been creating all afternoon. She got up, brushed the dirt off her knees, and walked gloomily halfway back to her mudhole. After sticking her tongue out at Alphonse's prickly head, she spiralled prettily into the grass and began to count. She had only counted eleven when new voices came from the hilltop. Géline's heart rallied and she peeked through the grass. Sure enough, Gabriel and Alphonse came walking down from their fort, arms held high. Behind them were Baptiste and Emilie, steadily pointing their guns.

"The fort is ours!" yelled Géline, running to meet them. "You said we'd never take it."

"And we did," tittered Emilie softly.

"And so what?" muttered Gabriel. "Three of you against two of us."

"But we have two girls!" said Géline.

"So?"

"So Alphonse was calling me a goose because I'm a girl," said Géline, eyeing Alphonse with murderous intent. "Our side had two gooses and only one boy. You had *two* boys, you goose!"

Gabriel burst out laughing and Alphonse shot him a dirty look. Baptiste and even Emilie joined in the laughter. But before anyone knew what had happened, Gabriel had snatched Baptiste's long, curved weapon from his grasp and was bolting down the hill, followed by Alphonse.

"Give me my musket!" yelled Baptiste, taking up the chase.

Géline and Emilie were close behind.

"Death to the mercenaries!" hollered Géline, pressing herself to a wild gallop down the hill.

"Shhh, cross your heart and say you're sorry!" shouted Gabriel over his shoulder as he raced toward the dykes.

"I can say it if I want."

"It's a swearword," he panted. "Only Satan would say it."

"No, it's not," broke in Alphonse to his fellow runaway.

"Yes it is!"

"I know what it means."

"Mercenary is a swearword."

They were running along the top of the dyke now. On one side was the wide spread of golden flax. On the other, looming higher than the grain, the glittering waters of Minas leaned on the dyke, ready to flood the Acadian farmlands. Alphonse was first on the floodgates.

"We're not allowed," protested Baptiste.

Alphonse shouted over his shoulder. "Then run to Maman, Baptiste *le chien!*"

A deep blush settled under the sweat on Baptiste's face. *Le chien!* As Gabriel followed Alphonse over the aboiteaux, they turned and took a few potshots at their pursuers. Moments later, Baptiste and Géline were speeding across the timbered floodgates. But Baptiste was right! Each forbidden step burned like fire. And Emilie stayed behind. She looked so little and lost, turning slowly to make her way home.

Géline's eye darted guiltily into the distance where the steeple of Grand-Pré basked in the sun. Her papa had helped drive these poles into the mud when the old floodgate broke. She was very little then, younger than Emilie, and the bulging vein in his neck had frightened her. But he had turned to her with a smile, "There, that should hold it. Just remember, Géline, it's not safe for little tadpoles. Don't ever let me catch you out here!" He didn't limp then, she remembered. And that was only three summers ago.

Down below, she caught a glint of seeping water on the dank timbers of the gate. "To this point but no farther," she recalled as she jumped off the far end of the aboiteaux to follow Baptiste along the level top of the dyke. Gabriel and Alphonse had already vanished into the forbidden forest.

2

IT WAS VERY STILL among the trees. A trace of decay and sweet sap invaded her nostrils. Her head cleared as she tried to penetrate the shade. This was the big capture. Baptiste was on his hands and knees behind a clump of ferns. No trace of the others, of course. But she wasn't taking any chances. She crawled through the underbrush, stepping carefully around twigs and branches. This would be easy. Alphonse had a noisy mouth and feet to match! But Gabriel could be tricky. He told her he'd gone tracking with Wabeyu and the other Mi'kmaq boys in the spring. But maybe he'd just made it up. Papa Basil wouldn't have let him go just like that!

A nearby branch snapped like a slap that turned her head. With a rush of triump she rose to her feet, aiming the gun at the unsuspecting enemy. As the bushes parted, her jaw dropped, the order to surrender freezing on her lips. Only a stone's throw away, the greenery was being brushed aside by broad-chested horses. Their hoofs sank into the yellowed pine needles on the path. Heavy black boots rode loosely in the stirrups, swinging to the leisurely stride of the horses. The saddles grumbled creakily in the silence. A dozen or more of King George's soldiers, bayonets at their sides, and backs erect against the rolling lilt of the animals. Géline was too struck to move. All they had to do was turn their heads. But if she tried to duck, it might draw their attention even sooner. So, like an abandoned statue, her wooden stick levelled at the passing redcoats and her head tingling with pungent horses' leather, she stood her ground.

She now realized where Alphonse and Gabriel had gone so fast! Across from her, behind the soldiers, Gabriel was perched halfway up an old maple tree, staring over at her with mute messages of caution. She must have looked a sight, because Gabriel's face soon broke into twitches of irrepressible laughter. Géline's blood ran cold as she watched him bobbing uncontrollably on the branch. They would surely hear him! So she gathered all her strength for a snake-like flash into cover among the ferns. But in the next instant she heard the guns being cocked and could see the redcoats halt their animals and stare in her direction. The pit of her stomach felt queasy. The front rider spoke softly and quickly to his men, but she didn't know many of their words. Two of them turned and came riding toward her, their bayonets at the ready. But from on high broke Gabriel's voice.

"By the grace of Mary mother of God, we surrender!"

The redcoats swung in their saddles, pointing their barrels at Gabriel, who had all he could do to hang on to the tree trunk. A moment passed. The redcoats peered at each other uneasily. Then the front rider broke into a chuckle and his companions followed suit. All fourteen of them laughed derisively. Gabriel cowered on his branch, tears wetting his cheek. Alphonse appeared from behind a rock and Baptiste was standing in ferns up to his knees.

"Bam!" said the front rider, pointing his finger at Baptiste. "Bam-bam!"

Baptiste couldn't decide whether to laugh or run.

"Bam-bam!" laughed the front rider, pointing at the stick in Géline's hand.

A young soldier bent toward her, offering his musket. The massive bulk of the butt approached her face. His

officer snapped sharply at him and the soldier pulled his weapon back onto the saddle. All was still. A cautious breeze stole through the silence. Baptiste hadn't figured out if he was going to be shot or not. The front rider gazed long and hard at the children, his brow heavy with thought. At length, his smile returned.

"*Bam!*" He aimed his finger at Alphonse.

"*P'choo!*" replied Alphonse.

"*Bam!*"

"*P'choo-p'choo!*"

And far across the fields rang the bell from Grand-Pré, a slow, melodious call to worship.

"The Angelus," whispered Baptiste, hearing the bell.

The redcoats touched their spurs to the horses and rode on, smiling and wagging their heads. She watched the grizzled hair-braids bobbing on their broad backs. Their big boots gently urged the horses forward. A harness rattled at the front, then another from somewhere near the back. Géline gave a shudder. They stared until the riders were gone, lost in the lush greenery as magically as they had appeared. Baptiste and Alphonse were already starting down to the dyke.

"Were you afraid?" said Géline.

"Me? Psh, I don't mind," answered Gabriel, quickly brushing a hand across his moist cheek.

They walked out into the sunshine together.

"Mercenary is a swearword."

"No, Gabriel. It's when you do something for coins even if you don't like it."

"See, I told you it was bad," said Gabriel, waving his arm. "You'd better hurry. Your papa is waiting for his supper."

She raced him to the aboiteaux.

3

THE SUN WAS ALMOST touching the weathercock on the barn when Géline came up through the orchard. Beside the well the horses were frolicking at their trough, so she tiptoed safely up the path and slipped into the shadow of the old willow tree by Papa's porch. By peeking around the gnarly trunk, she could look through the doorway. From the shadows came Papa's voice, good-natured and intent on the matter at hand. She couldn't quite decide what was being discussed, but now she heard the louder voice of the blacksmith answering.

"My friend, you're always in good spirits, when others are filled with gloom. No one sleeps easy at night. It's been six moons now."

"And another six will pass. Basile, our place is here. We've nothing to fear. We mind our own business. Let them cut each other's throats...."

Géline was sliding like a shadow along the wall. If she could only get upstairs, she'd jump into her cot and pretend that their loud words had wakened her. That would be a better excuse for leaving Papa without his supper!

"Shhh!" Their conversation came suddenly to a halt.

All was quiet, except for the measured motion of the ticking clock.

"I thought I heard a little ghost."

Of course! Monsieur Basile wasn't as deaf as her papa. She pressed herself breathlessly against the timbered wall. The old elbow-chair creaked and Basile the blacksmith showed his broad, whiskered countenance. The other chair followed suit, as Papa Bénédicte leaned forward to get a look at her.

"Géline?"

"Papa."

Behind them the fire cast a glow through the old man's snowy locks. Along the wall their huge shadows darted mockingly, and the pewter plates on the sideboard caught and reflected the flame, like shields of armies.

"Monsieur Basile and I have talking to do. But I'll have a word or two for you later. Now hurry and bring Monsieur Basile a pipe. And don't forget the bread for the Feast of Sainte-Eulalie. It's tomorrow!"

"Yes, Papa."

She hurried to the sideboard and brought the pipe and the leather pouch of tobacco for Basile. He took them with a contented grunt and winked at her kindly. Papa was staring into the fire.

"We'll farm," he continued. "We'll go fishing and hunting. We don't need them. The good Lord provides all that we need. Let's remember Him and thank Him."

And blah-blah-blah, thought Géline as she arranged the wooden vats on the workbench by the hearth. The old man crossed himself and peered reassured through the shadows in the ceiling.

"I was talking to my cousin a fortnight ago." Basile leaned forward, planting an elbow on his knee. "You know, Maurice in Upper Dyke, who left his farm to move over with the French at Beauséjour?"

Bénédicte nodded. Basile took a long, slow draft of his pipe.

"Well, he's not too happy."

"What is it?"

"You know Maurice. He wants to farm. He doesn't want to fight."

Bénédicte was still nodding. Géline's water splashed loudly into the trough, and she plunged her fingers into the sticky batter.

"So Maurice wouldn't go when they wanted him for the militia. But the governor in Quebec says Maurice is a rebel to the orders of the King. They took his farm away. Now he's got nowhere to farm."

Géline looked up from her work. Papa was staring into the embers.

"Maurice is not a coward," he said. "He's an Acadian! There isn't one of us who would join their mercenaries."

See, it's not a swearword, she thought, *or Papa wouldn't be using it!*

"But how can we say no? We gave most of our weapons away so we wouldn't have to sign the oath to fight for England. All we have is my hammer and the scythes in your barn."

"The redcoats are busy in Halifax. They haven't been out this way since the New Year. Believe it, Basile, we're safer unarmed, in the midst of our flocks and our barley, safer within these peaceful dykes besieged by the ocean, than the English and French in their forts, besieged by each other's cannon. Fear no evil, my friend."

Géline's hands worked the dough quickly, expertly. She remembered the heavy black boots riding loosely in the stirrups, bayonets at the ready, the rousing smell of leather. She could see the young soldier's smile and the butt of the musket close to her chin. *"They haven't been out this way since the New Year."* Papa didn't know. But she had seen them. They had all seen them. And Papa didn't know. A great noise broke her thoughts.

"God's name!" roared Basile, rising from his chair. "Louisbourg is not forgotten, nor Port Royal! Must we always bow to those who kick us? Daily injustice is done, and might is the right of the strongest! The Crown of France calls us traitors. Abbé Le Loutre is turning the Mi'kmaq against us. They've been stealing our animals! Governor Cornwallis wanted our signatures last summer! How can you sit so still?"

Bénédicte met his gaze, not unkindly, but without a word.

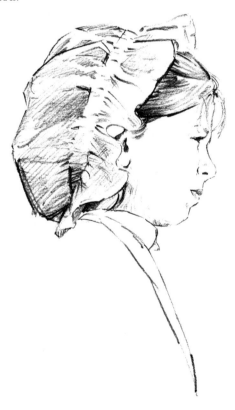

"Fine, I can't talk to you, Bénédicte. Something's come between us." He stomped to the door, and turned. "And no son of mine is going to marry an infidel's daughter! You can find another boy for Géline."

She heard his angry steps on the path. A moth was whirring at the lantern on the table. The clock was clicking. Bénédicte had slumped in his chair, his oak-brown face drawn into a mask of pain. It was a while before Géline could speak. Her words were soft, but very clear.

"I think Maman is watching. And it makes her sad."

Bénédicte turned on her. "Now what's this! That little neck is getting mighty stiff, Géline."

"I guess I'm Maman's girl."

He was wagging a crooked finger at her. "Remember who is head of this house."

"Maman."

Bénédicte rose from his chair in a rage. He stared at her while she stubbornly worked the dough. Something in him softened as he beheld her eyes, dark as a ripened cherry, and her brown tresses tucked under the white Norman cap. He huffed something unintelligible, turned and shuffled out of the door.

4

FROM THAT DAY, Father Félicien had strict orders to keep Géline away from Gabriel. Their papas were well thought of in the village and didn't flaunt their quarrel in public. But the word got around. It jumped gingerly from puckered lips into eager ears: at the laundry, at the potluck, at the milking, at the horse races, at the harvest, after church (or even during), and, of course, at the supper table. Soon every man, woman, and child in Grand-Pré knew. It wasn't really a topic for conversation, but everyone knew. And everyone knew where they stood, closer to Basile or closer to Bénédicte. The two papas carried on with their jobs for the winter. Months passed into years but there was nothing more to be said, so long as Father Félicien kept Gabriel and Géline in opposite corners of his class.

Every spring they moved outdoors. Father Félicien waddled about, looking for a level spot in which to set his elbow-chair. Géline hustled Thérèse and Emilie and a few others to a quick game of hopscotch, while the good Father was puttering with chalk, slate, and abacus. The boys glowered longingly at the girls' merriment.

"Come now, children, come, come!" called Father Félicien, clapping his sausage-fingered hands and collapsing contentedly on his chair. "Gabriel!"

The boy needed only this reminder to scurry as far from Géline as he could get.

"Let us pray."

The children sat on the grass, as the Father opened his black book.

"Holy Father, let the kingdom come in Your name. Give each new day Your blessing and food for our table...."

Catechism came first each morning, and Father Félicien's droning syllables mingled with the chatter of the chickadees and the woodpeckers. Lots of woodpeckers this year, thought Géline. They were drumming up a storm, twittering to each other in secret code. From where they were sitting, on the north embankment of the church, she could look out on the flats and the dykes. Far to the north rose Blomidon, crowned with mists from the open sea. But rarely would those touch the shores of home. She could count seven of the aboiteaux, their sluicegates half opened by last week's rainwater draining slowly into the Basin. The waters wandered at will, coiled like glistening serpents through the farmland. It was time to sow. She was hoping Papa would send her down with flagons of ale for the sowers. She hadn't forgotten their brown, sweaty faces gulping her ale under the midday sun. *Bless this girl!* they had sung to her. *She's the sunshine of Sainte-Eulalie!*

"And what is her special gift to us?" asked Father Félicien, pointing a chubby finger at Baptiste.

Baptiste hunched a little forward as the class turned to him for an answer. His cheeks and forehead turned their customary shade of pink. He shook his head. Alphonse had his hand up.

"Alphonse?"

"Father, her sunshine loads the orchard with apples."

Father Félicien nodded his pleasure. But now Géline jumped in.

"I know, I know, Father!"

"Yes?"

"It must be Sainte-Eulalie!"

All the children turned to her, their faces bright with amusement. *What?* she thought. *It has to be right! If anyone should know, I ought to.*

"Yes, Géline," spoke the Father with a stern edge to his words. "And if your ears had been here on the hill with us you would've heard us naming Eulalie over and over. That was not my question."

Everyone burst into a flood of cruel laughter. Father Félicien's little peppercorn eyes rested steadily on her. She must have turned as red as Baptiste *le chien*.

Géline edged the pail a bit forward. Old Loulou was happy to feel the fingers take hold of her udder and start the rhythmic pumping into the pail. The first spurts of milk bounced loudly on the bottom and the sweetness touched her nostrils, mingling with the straw, the manure, and the goldenrod by the side of the barn. Just get her started and that old Loulou would almost milk herself!

Lettering was fun! They had learned three more letters after lunch. That's when she liked Father Félicien the most. When he helped her spell words. He had promised to teach them all their letters by midsummer. She could write g-a-b-r-i..., but she knew she mustn't show him. He might tell Papa. She pursed her lips and whistled at Bijou, her snow-white heifer, who wore the herd's bell for the summer. Bijou was her favourite because she would come when Géline whistled. She poked her broad, moist muzzle into Géline's neck, almost nudging her off the milking stool.

"Bijou is such a silly girl, silly girl, silly girl," chanted Géline in time with the strokes of her milking.

Then came another whistle. Géline stopped short. She peered all around the barn, where the cows were shifting impatiently with the weight in their udders. Through the gaping doorway she could see one of Papa's broad-wheeled wains, empty and leaning its shanks on the straw-littered ground. Above her was the great, shaded dome of the rafters. Again the whistle! Her eyes followed it to the hayloft. *Mon Dieu*, Gabriel! He was flat on his belly at the edge of the loft, beckoning her to the ladder. She peered through the barn door again. No sign of Papa.

"You crazy fool, you!" she whispered hoarsely.

"What did you say?" he called down.

"Shhh!" she hissed at him and let go of old Loulou.

In a flash, she was at the ladder and climbing quickly toward Gabriel's grinning face.

GELINE HELD HIS HAND to steady herself on a rafter. In the steep shadows below, Papa's harrow was parked against a post, baring its wooden fangs in a wide, jawless grin.

"Where are you going?" he asked.

"Let's find the pearly stone."

"What for?"

"For good luck. Don't you know? The swallow brings a pearly stone from the beach to make her babies open their eyes and fly."

Gabriel made a face. "So?"

"What if the pearly stone can open anybody's eyes! Then our papas would become friends again."

"That would take more than a stupid stone."

Gabriel tucked his maman's jug in the crook of his arm. He stepped gingerly onto the high rafter, careful not to look down. The arches of his feet were tingling with dread.

Géline smiled. "Want to go back?"

"Me?" He shrugged. "Psh, I don't mind."

"You can leave the syrup in the loft."

That was all the reason he needed. With one hand clenching the jug as if it could save him from falling, he turned and made his way sloth-like back to the safety of the loft. From the edge, he could watch her crouching on the rafter. Her kirtle was draped smoothly over her toes, covering the rafter. The effect was magic. She was a hovering spirit of the air, reaching regally into the swallow's nest.

"Is it the pearly stone?" he asked excitedly.

Géline gave a snort. "It's an egg."

He broke into a chuckle.

"Oh, Gabriel, you're always laughing."

"Because you're funny."

"But you're making fun!"

He stopped giggling and shook his head slowly. They eyed each other.

"I should get home," said Gabriel.

"What about Angels?"

"But Maman wants her syrup."

"Give me a taste."

He uncorked the jug and she stuck in her finger.

"Mmmm," she crooned, licking it clean. "Be Angels with me."

So they sat side by side against a mound of hay, the jug wedged between Gabriel's thighs. He pulled out a straw and started chewing it. From overhead, a slender shaft of sunlight peeked into the dusky loft, gilding Gabriel's straw in a swirling, dizzying dance of dust. A sudden whir of wings announced a mother's return to one of the nests. Had she brought the pearly stone? Each of them wondered if the other had the same thought. And softly through the rafters, a salty breeze enveloped them with calm.

"I have to go," whispered Gabriel at length.

Géline stuck her finger in the syrup jug for more. Licking her mouth, she offered him a taste from her finger. He leaned a little forward, cleared his throat, took a lick. It was thick and sweet.

"I can't be Angels with Thérèse or Pauline," she said, tilting the jug forward to fill the bottom of her cupped hand, "or anybody." She sipped some, then held it out

for him. "I tried, but ... no. Just you ... are the only one."

Gabriel put his hands behind his back and craned his neck to lick the slippery syrup from her skin.

"I grow wings," she told him. "Like I'm free. Like the candles at church, burning so slowly. So deep and true. My heart is an angel."

The breeze hung softly in the wake of her words. Gabriel wasn't breathing right. After several moments, he found his voice again.

"Sometimes you're a little stupid," he muttered, licking his mouth.

"It's the truth, Gabriel!" She licked the last off her fingers. "Just because something is secret doesn't make it stupid."

"What secret?"

"Angels."

They sat side by side in a silence.

"We have to think of a plan," he said at last.

"What?"

"So we don't have to hide."

"Why won't your papa talk to my papa?"

He scratched his head, blinking up into the swirling dust.

"I guess it's on account of the English."

That's as far as he got. They jumped at the scratch of a boot in the doorway.

"Géline?" came the familiar voice.

Through a chink in the boards, they could see old Bénédicte giving Loulou an affectionate pat and reaching for the milk pail. He straightened up and gazed all around.

"Géline!"

She nudged Gabriel and whispered. "Talk to Papa. I dare you. Talk to him right now!"

"Are you serious?" He took one look at her.

She certainly was.

BENEDICTE STATIONED HIMSELF in the great portal of the barn door, pail in hand, and roared, *"Evangéline!"*

Anger did not come easily or often to Papa, but if she crossed him long enough, then it followed as night follows day. Still, his only answer came from the unmilked cows. He gave the doorsill an angry kick and hobbled off into the yard with hens clucking, squawking, and flapping at his feet. It was, perhaps, a good thing that the barnyard was such a carnival. In all the noise, Bénédicte had no reason to look back over his shoulder. Had he done so, he would have seen the skulking figure of Gabriel descending the outside stairs from the loft. As the old man made his way toward the root cellar, Gabriel followed like a haunted spirit, veering toward the orchard to cover his tracks.

"Good Monsieur."

Bénédicte came to a halt.

"A good evening to you, Monsieur."

He knew that voice all too well. It was Gabriel coming up the path. Bénédicte gazed under his bushy eyebrows at the gangly boy.

"Good, is it?" He turned toward the hill and opened his mouth wide. *"Evangéline!"*

They both stood there, listening for an answer.

"Is she lost?" ventured Gabriel at last.

"Evangéline!" yelled Bénédicte and headed for the root cellar.

Gabriel scampered along beside him.

"I've been thinking, Monsieur…"

"What?"

"I said I've been thinking…"

"That's rare!"

"Well, you see, Monsieur…"

"*Evangéline!*"

Gabriel listened respectfully along with the old man. Even the chickens were listening.

"See, what I had in mind…."

"You did?"

"Monsieur?"

"Basile's boy has something in mind? Ah well, better something than nothing."

Gabriel felt the jab deep in the pit of his stomach. Bénédicte trudged on, but Gabriel dogged his heels.

"I want no harm, Monsieur. Just your patience while I…."

"*Evangéline!*"

"That's right, Monsieur."

Bénédicte stopped and looked him in the eye.

"That's it. I wanted to ask about…."

"*Evangéline!*" he roared again, and the bulging vein in his neck made Gabriel think of a cobra.

"Géline, yes," he whispered, his hand picking fiercely at his leg. "That's what I…."

"Don't even think it!"

Gabriel bit his tongue. They stood silently in the still air. Gabriel felt drained. At length, he found his hands again and extended the syrup jug to Bénédicte.

"Monsieur, I have a favour to ask of you…."

"Is this from Basile?"

Gabriel hesitated, then shook his head truthfully.

"My daughter's hand?"

Gabriel stared. How could old folks know so much before you even told them?

"Through the honour of your daughter, Monsieur, to enter your family, Monsieur."

Bénédicte peered at him sternly. He couldn't let on that he was having a good chuckle to himself. The boy had only seen fourteen summers or so, but old Josephine had him well groomed for courtship!

"Through my daughter, eh?"

"Monsieur." Gabriel swallowed with difficulty.

"The son of a warmonger."

"Monsieur...."

"An infection in the blood of Acadie."

"You're not so clean yourself, living on the spoils of the land with no care for the dangers of tomorrow...." Gabriel caught himself, his eyes stinging.

He knew he had lost. He lowered his gaze under Bénédicte's grave scrutiny.

Aha, thought the old man. *From the horse's mouth! That's how they're talking in the blacksmith's kitchen. Perhaps the other kitchens too!* Bénédicte didn't bother with the root cellar. He didn't even call out for Géline again. He had all he could do to put one foot in front of the other back to his kitchen door.

Gabriel turned and ran for home. At the corner of the barn, he bumped into Géline.

"Well?"

He caught the twinkle in her eye. She must have been watching.

"I had him in my hand. He said he'd think about it."

Géline burst out laughing. He wiped his eyes.

"You had to go and spoil it."

"But look at all the bull I had to listen to."

"And of course you had to do the same thing!"

"He was calling us names! Warmonger! Wait till Papa finds out."

"No, Gabriel." She had a hold of his arm. "No! There are better ways. I have the gift of reasoning. You have your papa's temper. You ruined everything. But I'm going to the smithy to talk some sense with your maman and papa. Maybe when the weather gets cooler. Stand by the window! You might learn something. I'll have your papa soft as the red iron in his forge."

She leaned forward and touched her lips to his eye. Then she was running after Papa.

7

BAPTISTE LOOKED UP from his arithmetic and saw the geese. Streamers of wild geese trailing through the leaden sky, winging their way from ice-bound bays to the shores of tropical islands. As they approached, their mournful, honking salute descended upon the thatch roofs. The entire class turned their squinting faces to the sky. "As far away as the Indies," Father Félicien had told them. Thousands and thousands of miles. But they would always find their way back. They stretch their necks into the wind and go, safe in the hand of God. Each year something went with them. As they soared overhead, they plucked the last crumbs of summer from the shores of Acadie.

"Well, well," grunted Father Félicien from his chair, "tomorrow we'll go indoors."

Baptiste hung his head. It seemed as if only yesterday they had kicked off their heavy shoes for the summer. His feet had made friends with the grass. He peeked over at Géline, who was gazing dreamily after the geese. A few soft tendrils of her hair had come loose and fluttered lazily about her ear. Her neck was so thin, just like her papa's, but proud. Just like his. He liked to look at her. She made him feel better.

Now the season had returned, when the nights grew colder and longer. On the way home from class, they met the great rumbling wains returning from the fields, laden with briny hay, its fresh-cut odour wafting everywhere.

"It's a cold winter coming," said Baptiste.

"How do you know?" asked Géline.

"Papa told me. He can tell by the clover. And besides, the bees made too much honey."

Baptiste's papa was the notary, Monsieur LeBlanc. He reminded Géline of a stick of driftwood. But she'd never tell Baptiste that. She could listen forever to his stories. Every winter, they would stop off after school for a cup of hot cider and a good story at Baptiste's house.

"And I went hunting with Wabeyu and his big brother," said Gabriel. "We saw a fox at Melanson and you should've seen the fur on it!"

"See, then it's true!" said Baptiste proudly. "Fur means snow."

Géline stared glumly in front of her.

"Just think, we can get out the sleds," said Baptiste, wanting to see her smile.

But she didn't.

"Are you coming in for a story?" asked Baptiste as he turned in through the squeaky gate.

Géline shook her head. "I've got things to do before milking."

Gabriel looked over at her, puzzled.

"See you tomorrow then," smiled Baptiste.

"See you tomorrow," said Gabriel, and Géline waved as Baptiste walked down the little rutted path to the notary's front door.

They walked along with the cows. Old Charlot was bringing them back from pasture. The barns would be waiting, brimming with the winter's hay. Géline could guess how the herd was feeling as they pawed the

ground and rested their necks wistfully on each other,
their nostrils flaring with the crispness of autumn. They
would spend the cold season cooped up in their pen.
The comfort of each other's warmth couldn't quite
make up for the loss of summer's adventure. She ran
to the front of the herd and walked with her arm
around little Bijou's white neck. Bijou seemed happy
enough, trotting in front with the brass bell tinkling
from her collar.

"Papa never knew about the mercenaries," said
Géline.

Gabriel was talking with Charlot.

"What?" He came running up behind her, his hand
resting on Bijou's back. "What?"

"Do you remember three summers ago? We had that
fort on the hill." Gabriel was nodding. "You saw the
redcoats, right?"

"Yeah, remember when I thought mercenary was a
swearword!" he laughed.

But Géline was serious.

"We all saw them."

"Yes, of course," said Gabriel.

"Papa doesn't know. He thinks the English only
come in the spring for the Council of Elders."

"So?"

"What do they want, riding so quietly in our forest?
I wanted to ask Papa."

"Yes, yes, you go ahead, Géline! Tell him that we
crossed the aboiteaux and he'll lock us in the root cellar."

Géline leaned her cheek on Bijou's head. They walked
silently.

"See you, Charlot," yelled Gabriel at last, at the turn-
off to the smithy. "See you tomorrow, Géline."

"No, wait." She let go of Bijou. "I'm coming with you."

"Are you crazy?"

"I told you, remember? Stand by the window and don't say a word."

"You *are* crazy!" smiled Gabriel, and his eyes were shining.

8

IN THE GATHERING DUSK, Basile's smithy seemed ready to burst with light. Always in the autumn, Géline and Gabriel had run straight from school to stand inside the door and watch with wonder, while Basile took a horse's hoof in his lap like a plaything, nailing the shoe in its place. Always in the autumn, until three summers ago. Nothing was the same now. Nothing was easy anymore.

As she neared the door, the evening rang with the powerful strokes from Basile's hammer. She glanced over at Gabriel who had stationed himself by the window where the smithy joined on to the house. He gave her the sign. When she stepped through the door, the heat swallowed her face like a blanket. With sudden gladness she savored the familiar fumes of melted iron. In the centre of Basile's shop stood the well-used anvil. That was where she and Gabriel liked to huddle, safe from blizzard or frost, to watch the laboring bellows. As the sparks expired into ashes, Basile would poke them lightly with his boot and laugh, "Look at the pretty nuns, going off to chapel!"

He was hard at work now, his massive arm wielding the hammer to shape a smoking cartwheel tire. Another one lay nearby, like a fiery snake coiled in a circle of cinders. Basile looked over and she curtsied, smiling. He went back to swinging his hammer. Through the grimy window, Gabriel was urging her on. She curtsied again, but Basile ignored her. Instead he showered the twilight with sparks as he coaxed another sizzling snake from the fire onto the floor.

"Nothing better to do?" he shouted over the bellows.

She curtsied again, lowering her eyes to the floor. He put down his hammer and let go of the bellows. As its panting ceased, he grumbled, "Well, what is it?"

"You're so busy, Monsieur Basile."

Basile looked at her blankly, looked at his anvil, shrugged his shoulders.

"We were talking at the well," she went on, "and someone said you're the best blacksmith in Acadie."

His face brightened.

"Yes, Monsieur, and they said there's none better in Halifax!"

"Who was it said that?" he asked, his big face beaming.

"Who?" Géline felt flushed. "Uh ... let me think.... Oh yes ... it was.... Too bad, I can't remember."

Out of the corner of her eye she could see Gabriel's blurry grin against the window pane. Basile wiped his hands on the leather apron.

"Huh! Well, I guess word gets around!"

Through the door at the back came another voice, cutting through all else.

"Who are you talking to, Basile?"

He gave a flustered snort.

"Uh ... no one, my *belle*. No one at all."

But that was not so wise, for in the next instant Joséphine stood in the doorway. Her chin had stationed itself habitually a step ahead of the rest of her face, and although she was now shorter than Géline, her eyes were quick enough for both of them.

"Aha! No one at all." She spoke like a woodpecker. "It's a good thing I have my wits, because yours are out when they need to be in. That girl's got her claw in you." Her words fell crisply like slate shingles on a stone slab.

Géline curtsied quickly, smiling all the while.

"I told Monsieur Basile he's famous in the land and his name is respected. And surely, Madame, the same may be said of you."

Joséphine dug her hands into her sides and spread her elbows like a courting woodgrouse. "Our name is good, yes. That's nothing new. Lajeunesse is a very good name. Very good. Not like some."

Géline took a deep breath. "So, I've come to speak with two people of such good name and respect."

"Well, you'd better make it quick," was Joséphine's reply, "because we've got work to do. We can't sit around all day. Like some."

Swallowing her pride, Géline forged ahead.

"Madame Joséphine and Monsieur Basile, seeing how the times are full of care and worry with England and France and the Mi'kmaq and the soldiers coming in from everywhere and...."

"Yes?" snapped Joséphine curtly, taking the wind out of Géline's sails.

Géline caught a glimpse of Gabriel shaking with laughter. Nothing was going to stop her now!

"Well, it's a troubled time to be Acadian and the Lord says we should love one another. Don't you see? If we can't love the English or the French or anybody else, we'll just have to love each other. So that's why I've come to you, Madame and Monsieur." She paused, catching her breath. Joséphine's eyes had narrowed. "To make a peace with you. To make friends, so Gabriel can have me for his wife."

They stared in disbelief. Basile was opening his mouth to speak, when Joséphine snapped in.

"*Never!*"

She turned to leave, but Géline wasn't about to let her. "Are you going to step into your grave saying *never*?"

Joséphine turned and looked her square in the eye. Géline tried to muster a smile, but it wasn't there. Basile had his mouth open wide to speak, but too late.

"I know his kind," shrugged Joséphine. "My Basile told me. Your papa is going to let the English have Acadie."

Géline felt the blood pushing at her temples. The hurt was tugging at all the muscles of her face.

"It's a wonder you could give birth to Gabriel, Madame, because I'd swear you're a man."

"A what?" she hissed and stepped closer.

"A man! One of them." Basile tried to protest, but too late. Géline was on fire. "Yes, he's just as bull-headed as my papa. And you, you have none of the love that the Lord gave to women. Everyone is fighting all around Acadie and we're trying to get a little peace. But you bring the wars right into our own midst. Shame on you, Joséphine! Shame on you, woman of Acadie!"

Joséphine's mouth was hanging open, ready to do battle. But no words would come out. Basile stood like a tree struck by lightning. Géline saw them in a blur, as tears washed into her mouth. She turned and ran for the door.

BIJOU IS BURNING! Géline sat bolt upright. *The cows are burning!* How could they be? She'd seen it. But how could they? Bijou's naked, bulbous eye scorched with flame! Géline's whole frame was shaking with grief. Bijou's moist muzzle crashing onto the splintered floorboards! It was an evil dream. So evil that it wouldn't let go of her. She saw the flames! She saw them even now. Between the white curtains of her little window, the sky was red. She rubbed her eyes and looked again. The window was not dark. It was burning! *Mon Dieu*, it was burning! It was fire. She rubbed her eyes again. She was wide awake, and it was fire.

"Over here!" she heard Papa shouting. "I've got water!"

"No!" she cried out and lunged forward to look out.

She tried to get a clear view through the window. Grabbing her quilt against the cold, she stumbled out of her room and onto the landing, past Papa's open door, down the noisy stairs, out onto the front step.

The night was crazed with alarm. Men were scrambling across the yard with buckets and barrels of water, yelling to each other, splashing and pelting their spill into the snow. She wrapped herself tight. Now she could hear the dream again, that eerie, wailing squeal of frenzied animals. Clutching the doorpost, she gazed over to the north barn and, with a hard knot in her throat, saw the shadowy gables safe in darkness. Great sobs of relief burst from her body. Bijou! Bijou was just a bad dream. But on the other side of the orchard, flames were towering madly into the night. It wasn't Papa's barn.

"It's Normand. Damnation, he'll lose them all!" came Papa's voice from the darkness.

Alphonse's house! And Papa was swearing! She saw him walking up from the well. He was stooping, winded, overcome. He was stumbling in the snowy sludge. Behind him were Gérard-in-the-bush and Charlot, hobbling down the hill with water bouncing from their buckets. Alphonse came stumbling to the well to fill up. He was shaking his head and whining strangely. She couldn't tell who the others were. Basile came storming forward with a large barrel on his shoulder.

"It could be Le Loutre!" he yelled.

Bénédicte stopped in his tracks and looked back toward the blacksmith. "Abbé Le Loutre from France?"

Basile was fiercely hauling in the rope to bring his bucket out of the well.

"He doesn't heed King Louis now. He's nobody's servant! He burned the church at Beaubassin just to make us fight."

"Yes," answered Papa. "It could be."

"He's gone in the head, like a jackass," thundered Basile as he tipped the bucket into his barrel.

"Have they got the water wagon out?" yelled Bénédicte.

Basile was rushing off with his water. "They've drained it already! They're up at west dyke, but the tide isn't in yet!" he called and was gone into the night.

Bénédicte stumbled past Géline and threw the door shut. "C'mon, girl, this is not for you. Up to bed!"

"I can't sleep," she moaned. "All Alphonse's cows...."

Bénédicte nodded, collapsing in his elbow-chair. "I think they'll save some."

Géline hurried to the hearth and struck one of the long matches, kindling the dried bark and moss. She laid a couple of logs over yesterday's coals.

"I heard about your bad manners," said Bénédicte, his voice low and serious as he stared at the little flickers on the hearth.

She looked at him, puzzled.

"I was talking to Basile," he added.

Géline couldn't find any words. She moved to the window and gazed across the orchard at the greater fire.

"It brings shame on my head," he continued.

"It was no worse than his own manners. Or Joséphine's. You bring shame on your own heads."

"And you should mind your manners!" growled Bénédicte, turning on her.

Papa's anger stabbed her deeply.

"How could I know! Why do you have to be old to yell and show your feelings, Papa? Why do I have to be the only one with manners?"

Something in his eye softened as he gazed at her, framed by the dark window. The glare from Normand's barn played vividly on her cheek. Her eyes were opened wide, her lips parted, hungry with confusion. He bowed his head, shaking the matted white locks.

"What's come over you, Géline? Is it Gabriel?"

She made no answer.

"Basile's boy! If the bay froze over, top to bottom, and then out to Ile Saint-Jean, and Basile underneath it all, you couldn't freeze that mouth of his!" He poked the fire, mumbling to himself. "His head is too hot. Must be from those ovens all day long. No one hoops a barrel as quick as he. He put those same tires on my wains before you were born! But now? I wouldn't let him straighten a nail for me."

"But you've been talking with him."

"Talking! Mary mother of God, who can talk? It's the boy I like." The flames were dancing in Papa's eyes. "Remember, that first New Year? It must be ten summers now." He slouched back in his chair, staring into the crackling fire. "I was so scared we'd have a woman knock at the door first thing. That would've sent me another year of bad luck. Wasted crops, a plague on the animals, or the barn on fire like Normand's—whatever the good Lord says. So I *sent* for good luck! I told Basile, would he send his boy over to knock on the door, and I'd give him a coin and some peanuts. So Gabriel came to the door, teeth rattling in his head, half asleep. And he was standing right there, by the fire, eating his peanuts and clutching his coin. For good luck!"

Géline was smiling. The gravelly good humour of her Papa's voice always made her feel safe.

"It was lucky for me," she said softly.

"You played together every summer. God's luckiest children."

A sudden tremor rocked the floorboards. The door flew open with a crash. Géline gasped, pressed against the window. Stumbling into the firelight, came two Mi'kmaq warriors supporting a black-robed stranger. One of the Mi'kmaq slammed the door behind them and turned a musket on Bénédicte. She knew him. It was Wabeyu's brother.

"What in the name of...?" gasped the old man, still in his chair.

"Shut your mouth or you'll die," hissed the other Mi'kmaw, as he helped the blackrobe to a chair.

"What do you want in my house?" growled Bénédicte.

But Wabeyu's brother strode quickly across the room and grabbed for Géline. She lunged for the stairs, but his arm was swift and strong. He swept her off balance and caught her around the neck, pressing the musket to her head.

"Papa," she whimpered, forcing her eyes shut.

Inside her eyelids, the heavy black boots flickered in their stirrups. The forbidden forest. She was seeing the young soldier's smile and the butt of his musket so close to her chin. But now it was a barrel's point, pressed cold into her ear.

10

THE BLACKROBE PULLED himself upright on his chair. Clasping the armrest, he met Bénédicte's eye.

"I come in the name of our Lord. But these twisted times force me to abuse your good charity."

At these words, Géline opened her eyes and observed the stranger. He had one hand pressed to his side. His eyes were glazed with exhaustion. From the yard came the abrupt beating of horses' hoofs.

"Nothing, sir! No one there," rang an English soldier's voice through the door.

Wabeyu's brother tightened his grip on her. The blackrobe met the other Mi'kmaw's fearful eye.

"Take a look on the dykes," came the answer outside. "I'll check the blacksmith's house. And don't forget, sergeant! Anyone who gives him shelter, will be shot as a traitor."

Géline's head was swimming. Everything was connecting now. She knew that voice. From where, she couldn't say. But the voice was deeply lodged in her memory. "*Anyone who gives him shelter....*" The blackrobe beckoned quickly to Wabeyu's brother and he gave her a shove into the room, forcing her directly toward the priest. She was swivelled off her feet and, despite her best efforts, landed on the stranger's knee, the blunt musket still nudging at her head. His arm reached around her.

"One false move and she's dead," spoke the blackrobe, and his breath brushed her hair and her cheek. "We need horses."

Papa was on the edge of his chair, his jaw working in mute rage. He looked little and forlorn on that side of the hearth. His oak-brown features were taut with conjecture, his bony hand clasping the armrest.

"Are you the Abbé from France?"

"Shhh!" hissed the blackrobe.

The other warrior slipped over to the door and stooped slightly to peer out through a chink. Around his waist, she discovered a belt hung with two scalps. She couldn't hold back a shudder. All was silent, except for the crackling fire and Papa's clicking clock. And, of course, the laboured breathing behind Géline's ear. It carried a piercing smell of strong herbs that prickled in her nose as he spoke. This was the man! The Abbé Le Loutre that Papa had spoken of so often.

Now the Mi'kmaw nodded to the blackrobe that the yard was clear. She felt his arm relax a little. But Wabeyu's brother still had the gun to her ear.

"I *was* the Abbé of Acadie, yes. For many years I tried. But I spit on your lazy lives and your flabby souls." The blackrobe clasped Wabeyu's brother by the shoulder. "These are my children. They know truth. They must survive the destruction."

"Don't hold so hard, I beg of you," pleaded Bénédicte hoarsely, his trembling hand reaching to Géline.

Le Loutre's grip stiffened around her ribs.

"Father, why have you turned against us?"

"I do not turn. But *you* have turned! You've all turned away and you'll roast forever in the pits of hell! I am the Word. The Lord Almighty is seated in my soul. I am a voice to His command."

Spiced and peppered! thought Géline, as he breathed heavily into her hair. The room was silent. The echo of Le Loutre's words danced grotesquely upon the walls.

Géline was dizzy. She listened for Papa's clock. She tried to hear the ticking. But the silence was so thick, the ticking was nowhere.

"The English have chased France from her old possessions," said Papa at last. "What can we do about that? We've refused to fight for them."

"You don't need a gun to kill," hissed Le Loutre in reply. "Your indifference kills! Your self-satisfied little farmer's prayer keeps you happy with your clods of cabbage and turnip. But, Monsieur...."

At the door, the Mi'kmaw hissed for silence. Outside, but farther away this time, the redcoats were shouting. *Anyone who gives him shelter will be shot,* remembered Géline with a chill. It was that voice again. But from where? And when? *Will be shot!*

She peered anxiously at Papa. His eyes were fixed on her, leaning forward with his elbows on his knees. Though no one else would've known, she knew her Papa's eyes so well that in the very heart of them, she saw him saying, *Just be patient, little tadpole, Papa loves you.* Géline smiled faintly. But Papa's face was set. She tried to get a look at Wabeyu's brother, but he kept the barrel hard against her cheek. That way he could hide his shame, was her guess.

There was the clock again, clicking in her ear. All was quiet outside. Le Loutre's head slumped on her shoulder, his breathing short and wheezy. The hand that had clasped his side dropped slowly into his lap; it was drenched with blood. Géline couldn't stop staring.

Wabeyu's brother spoke quickly to his companion in their own tongue. The other warrior left his post by the door and slipped the robe off Le Loutre's shoulders. The Abbé's arm released her long enough to slide out of the sleeve. Then the Mi'kmaw crouched beside her, pulling out his long knife. Her heart jumped into her throat as her eye caught the scalps on his belt. But instead he slit her skirt up the middle. Géline gasped for shame, but soon realized he wasn't going to hurt her. He tore a large piece of the cloth and began to bandage the slumping priest.

"These are the final days," resumed the blackrobe with some effort. "This is the light or the dark, Monsieur Cabbage! And we'll fight to survive. We must *fight*! We must stop the English! Make yourselves pure!" The Mi'kmaw was squatting to tie the bandage around his ribs. Le Loutre rested his hand on the warrior's shining head of hair. "Like them. They're losing their land to the English. They're losing the waters where they fish. They've lost the forest where their ancient loved ones dwell. And you? You bury your heads in the haystack and think you can mind your business." He pushed Géline off his knee onto the floor at his feet, where the musket's barrel guarded her closely. Le Loutre was looming over her, aiming at Bénédicte.

"I tell you, Monsieur, the Devil has pitched his tent in Acadie and you're all going to roast. Every one! Because you're not pure! The fire will purge you, yes it will. You'll be howling like those cows and the fire will gut you to the bone and then, *maybe* then, you'll begin to know purity! What it is to be wide awake, fully awake. To live with the terror."

His words left a numbed stillness in the room, mocked only by the soft flickering from the hearth. More noises sifted in from the yard; boots slogging through the sludge, Alphonse calling to his papa somewhere in the orchard. Géline closed her eyes. In that instant, she recalled the young soldier bending to her, offering his musket. The massive butt approaching her face. His officer snapping sharply at him and the soldier pulling his weapon back onto the saddle. His officer's voice. "*Bam!*" he had said, pointing his finger at Baptiste like a toy gun. And "*Bam-bam!*" pointing at the stick in Géline's hand. That was the voice. Three summers ago, and now he was in the yard.

She was wrenched from her musings by Papa's voice.

"He said he'd shoot anyone who gave you shelter. Father, show your mercy."

She looked up at Le Loutre. His features were glistening with sweat, a sickly pallor under the tanned skin, his eyes like embers glowing in the ashes of his face.

"Did you hear the screams, Father?" Papa's face was fast filling with rage. "Did you hear the torment of innocent creatures roasting in your fire?"

"No one is innocent anymore," groaned Le Loutre wearily. "Innocence is lost."

"Monsieur l'Abbé, I haven't studied in Paris like you. I don't know God except from Father Félicien and the rain that waters my field. But I know that God gives life, not death. When we're too old to live, it's God who stops giving. But to take life from the young is to serve the Devil. So we must refuse to fight the Devil's war. We must stick to the chores that God gave us to do."

Le Loutre was on his feet, leaning on the Mi'kmaq warrior, rising to his full height.

"Satan is here. *Satan!* That's the work God gave me to do! Do you suppose if Satan saw you working hard and steady in the field, he'd just pack his bags and leave? 'Ahhh, but Monsieur Cabbage is such a God-fearing man, I'd better get packing!' " Le Loutre snorted scornfully. "You're a blindman, Monsieur. All your days add up to nothing! Your lazy soul is a traitor to the Crown of France and the spirit of our Lord Father. I'll take away your priests. Father Félicien is ordered back to France. No one to pray for your soul. No one shall give you the last sacrament. No one shall bless the birth of your children. You've lost your church and your life eternal."

On Le Loutre's bandage, she could see the blood blooming darkly through her woollen cloth. Bénédicte had risen now, and Wabeyu's brother turned his gun on the old man.

"Monsieur l'Abbé, I look at you," he spoke, "and I wonder where is Satan? You've murdered innocents all over Acadie to make us fight. It was your orders to burn our homes at Beaubassin so we'd have to flee instead of mixing with redcoats. You've terrorized women and children, and massacred simple woodcutters. The Mi'kmaq do not thirst for blood. They never took a scalp until the Crown of France bought them with bribes."

Géline couldn't see for tears. Her head was whirling with faces from now and long ago. Papa's neck bulging so dangerously. The dark drip from Le Loutre's bandage plopping into her lap. Wabeyu's brother flashing his black eyes at her papa. Basil's shouting over on the other side. And now the horses were back. No voices this time. Just the hoofs galloping up the hill. Le Loutre spoke quietly with the Mi'kmaq in their own tongue, seemingly as comfortable with it as with French. They answered him, and Wabeyu's brother checked the chink at the door. Le Loutre spoke again, insistently. The other Mi'kmaw grumbled and nodded. Their quiet conference was cut short by the stabbing cry from a bugle, over toward Gabriel's house or the village green. Everyone stood transfixed, with bated breath. Again the bugle sounded. It was a call to summons, not their own salute but the Governor's.

Le Loutre turned to Bénédicte. "Go to your summons, old man."

Papa stared at him, confused.

"Go. Quickly! When you're gone, we'll go to the stables."

"I'll take my daughter," he said, and Géline ran to him, clasping her hand firmly in his. "I'll have my daughter!" he whispered, his eyes shiny as he squeezed her hand.

She slipped into her boots at the door. Papa helped her into the long-coat. They turned and looked once more upon the haggard Abbé, propped up by Wabeyu's proud brother. Then they pushed the door open and stepped into the snow.

11

THE FROSTY MORNING turned their breath to steam.
Along the road the snow had been beaten down by sleds
and horses, but there was a hint of ice and Papa's hand
sat heavier than usual on her shoulder. His limp got
worse when he was tired. She had never stayed up this
late, not even for the Mardi Gras, but he was too
preoccupied to notice. Not a word was spoken. Another
brief blast came from the bugle. As it faded, there was
only the monotonous crunch of their boots on the snow.
Day was breaking with a pale yawn across the bay of
Minas.

Emerging from the dark, Cape Blomidon floated
majestically on waves of vapor. The Chief Ulgimoo had
told Papa that long before the first Acadians came from
the shores of Normandie, Big Chief Glooscap had had
his wigwam on Cape Blomidon. Times would change,
but Glooscap would never forget his Mi'kmaq. No
matter how the tides of Minas came and went, Blomidon
would stand firm. Glooscap's messenger was the loon.
He was there this morning, somewhere on the misty
dyke, pitching his quizzical call against the stillness. But
silence returned quickly, like summer's grass reclaiming
the path to a fallow field.

In the growing light, they could see others on their
way to the summons. Just ahead was Monsieur Godin,
but no Emilie. Géline smiled to herself. Emilie was
surely asleep through it all. From everywhere, doors
were clunking and new bodies were joining the march
toward the green.

"Papa?"

His hand brushed her cheek. "Yes, my girl?"

"Does everyone have to go?"

"No. Only the deputies." He lifted his shoulders in despair. "Only the wise are fools enough to meet before breakfast."

Géline couldn't find words for all that was in her head. Thérèse's papa was walking up ahead and behind them came Gerard-in-the-bush, lugging the milk pail he had forgotten to set down before leaving home. Papa lurched sideways on a slick of ice and his strong, knobbly hand wrenched her off balance before he recovered.

"Papa?"

"What is it now?"

She could tell he was glad to have her safe, but also distraught with what lay ahead.

"Are the redcoats our enemies?"

"No." His brow was resolute. "No, they're not."

They passed Gabriel's house. Already Josephine had a thin wisp of smoke rising from the chimney. And there was smoke from some of the other homes too. They turned into the village street.

"Do they spy on us?"

"What?" Papa looked at her a moment. "Who?"

"The redcoats, Papa. The mercenaries!"

Bénédicte looked eastward. He knew the sun was up, but the sky was a thick pall of grey. Snow was in the air.

"No. Why should they? We signed their oath before you were born, swearing our allegiance so long as we don't have to fight. We can't harm anyone."

"But that priest says we can."

Papa gazed at her darkly.

"Monsieur l'Abbé said we can do harm if we don't help against the redcoats."

Papa's moustache was studded with tiny icicles as he spoke, looking ahead up the street.

"People who curse and swear can't bear those who don't," he said. "Géline, my girl, you'll see it every day. Thieves can't bear those who don't steal. So, also, those who fight can't bear those who won't."

Géline slipped her hand into Papa's and gently held it.

"So there's no danger in the woods, then?" she stammered at last.

Bénédicte shook his head, but not lightly.

"So then if I...." She choked on the words. "I'm old enough now. And Gabriel's allowed to go hunting. If I crossed the aboiteaux to the woods, would you let me?"

"Don't you dare."

"But Papa...."

"Hush now. I don't want my little tadpole wandering too far from home."

The deputies were in full attendance, except Denny-on-the-ridge who was visiting with his sister Marie on Ile Royale. They were all fairly old; they had to be to get on Council. The only one there of Géline's age was Alphonse. No one else had Papa's pressing reason to bring the family out-of-doors this morning. Alphonse looked a mess and was white as a ghost. His eyes were swollen from tears. It occurred to Géline, that it was probably more from smoke than from crying. Father Félicien wasn't there either. He wasn't supposed to be, because he was appointed by the Crown of France and not really an Acadian. That's what Papa had told her, and he was very particular about who attended the Council. But she couldn't see anything so different about the Father, except for the robe he wore.

The brash bugle pierced her thoughts. In the middle of the open green, a small troop of soldiers were waiting on horseback. The horses' nostrils were spouting steam as they shook their manes impatiently, their hoofs scraping into the snow. Géline held Papa's hand tightly as she walked closer, observing the soldiers' high boots in their stirrups and the double rows of brass buttons on their waistcoats.

"How many did you lose?" she heard Papa asking Normand.

Alphonse gazed at her and she tried to smile encouragingly. He just turned away and stepped behind his papa. Poor Alphonse.

"Five of the heifers and half a dozen turkeys," said Normand flatly.

"Lord bless you, Normand," answered Papa. "It's a crying shame. I've got a heifer I'll give you."

"Me too," came Basile's burly voice behind their shoulder.

"And you can take some of my chickens," croaked old Bernard-around-the-bend, laying his arthritic paw on Normand's shoulder.

Normand just looked at them and said nothing. His eyes spoke clearly.

Géline looked over at the English soldiers, sitting there so motionless, almost statues, except for their fidgeting, snorting animals. Couldn't they just get on with it! Her toes were freezing. Then she saw his face, flanked by the other soldiers. It was the front rider. Three summers ago in the forbidden forest.

Her heart jumped and she stepped quickly behind Basile, where she wouldn't be recognized. What if he told on her in front of Papa? Papa would lock her up for sure. He musn't find out. She wasn't anybody's tadpole anymore! And she was tired of these secrets. Papa ought to hear what her eyes had seen, and also what she wanted in her heart. She peered out from Basile's broad shadow toward the English horsemen. There he was, unfurling a parchment scroll while conferring with his uniformed interpreter. The interpreter turned toward them and cleared his throat.

"Good friends of Grand-Pré," he spoke with a curt, clipped accent, "who has seen Abbé Le Loutre?"

The deputies muttered among themselves. Géline felt the blood rising to her cheeks. She looked over at Papa. He was silent.

"Jean-Louis Le Loutre," resumed the interpreter. "Who can help us find him?"

The deputies were shaking their heads, glancing blankly at each other. Géline was too flushed to even look at Papa. His silence was choking her.

"Surely," went on the interpreter, "you're not protecting the lunatic who just killed half of Normand Cormier's stable? Don't forget, anyone who gives him shelter will be executed as a traitor."

Basile grunted angrily to himself. The morning sat drearily on the white rooftops. Across the road, the church looked unlike itself at this early hour. She could see the snow-covered slope where they would sit again in the spring with Father Félicien. He had even promised to help them learn English words, although it wasn't allowed. Maybe that's why the bleeding blackrobe had said he would send Father Félicien away forever.

Maybe she'd never learn English words!

"On behalf of His Majesty King George, I ask you again to swear a full and proper oath of allegiance to England."

The interpreter's words echoed in a great silence, as the deputies squinted at each other, squirming and shifting. Géline could see Alphonse sitting cross-legged on the ground, taking no part in what was happening.

"Good sir," came Basile's deep voice, "we and our fathers took your oath." He paused while the interpreter turned and spoke his words in English to the officer. "These several winters," he went on, "we've lived faithful and obedient, in spite of terror and threats."

The interpreter was translating again. The officer listened intently, his eyes pondering Basile's broad face. He quickly responded, and the interpreter turned to them again.

"Threats from whom?"

"Like this night. From the French and the Mi'kmaq too."

The English officer listened to Basile's reply. It was impossible to tell what he was thinking, or if he was thinking. His answer came calmly and methodically, although the interpreter spoke more quickly.

"But there is no middle. If you're British subjects, you must *fight* as any other. If you will not, then you are subject to the French and no longer in possession of your lands or your liberty. I order you here and now to sign the unqualified oath."

The interpreter took the scroll from his officer and poked it at Basile's shoulder. He made no motion to receive it.

"I say you're wrong, sir." Basile's voice had that same

throaty quaver which he had poured so liberally on her papa. "I say it was wrong to take our guns. They aren't a proof of anything. It's not the gun that will lead us to revolt. Taking it away will not make us more faithful. Only our clear conscience will make us keep your oath."

The interpreter had been keeping his officer abreast through Basile's rapid outpour. Now the officer replied, seemingly with weariness. The interpreter quoted him.

"What's your excuse, Monsieur Lajeunesse, for presuming to lecture the British Crown on the nature of fidelity?"

Géline felt Papa growing anxious, as he knew Basile's temper well. She knew it was time for him to do his work.

"Your Excellency," began Bénédicte, with a gracious sweep of his arm, "we are loath to test your patience further. But we must consult together as a group before we can sign. We beg your indulgence for such another limited term."

While his words were being reported to the officer, Géline began to step slowly back from the scene, step by step, away from her papa who was fully intent on the officer's face. No one seemed to notice as she turned and walked from the common. She had no clear purpose, but her feet were carrying her swiftly and her heart was racing with defiance. The road dipped toward the dykes. She wasn't anybody's tadpole any more!

12

THE WATERS NEVER FROZE. The tide came and went, shilly-shallying to and fro at the craggy heel of Blomidon. It kept the bay of Minas always open. Ice floes drifted and crunched; in the cracks, the water was black as death. Géline was in a hurry to nowhere, away from things she couldn't change. Inside the dyke, the fields were sleek with snow, spotted only with spears of brown straw. This was the way to the aboiteaux, to the forbidden forest. She didn't know what she'd do when she got there, but her heart was shouting. A chill stung her eyelash, then another her cheek. Snowflakes. Softly descending on them all, on Papa, on the soldiers, on Alphonse cross-legged and hunched over his new-found grief, and on Maman with her arms stretched by her side under the grass. Snow to cover the dirt. Snow to hush the world. More and more flakes, assailing her eyelids as she walked. But nothing would have stopped her.

Through half-closed eyes, she saw someone coming, stepping down from the aboiteaux. The floodgates, draped in frozen seepage, appeared to be sculpted in glass. He was fast approaching, a fur cap rammed over his eyes, and snugly wrapped in a woollen scarf. When he got quite near, she realized she'd have to step aside to dodge him. But he stepped with her, and now they were eye to eye. Gabriel! His eyes were smiling through the snowfall, fluttering as the flakes drove into his face. She almost lost her breath to see him. Here; now. He was handsome. And he was no longer a boy. Something had happened over the winter. Like the fox at Melanson that grew so much fur for the cold. Gabriel wasn't skinny any more. She saw his shoulders. The thick, dark curls in the nape of his neck were powdered with snow.

His gloved hand found her shoulder, then her hair. Gently he shook all the snow from her brown tresses and brushed the front of her coat. Then he slipped off the glove, and laid his warm hand against her snowy cheek. Her breathing was short and speechless. Her hands moved on their own, taking his bare fingers and pressing them to her cheek, his warmth rushing straight to her pounding heart. She brought his fingers to her lips and laid them across her mouth. And now his face, his nose nudging her eyebrow, his breath warming her skin. Géline was safe. She needed no one to show her happiness. It was here. It was he. Her lips were against his, curving and preciously seeking the most from his kiss. This was Gabriel, whose fur was thicker than the fox at Melanson, holding her with sinewy arms and feeding her kisses until her head was spinning and all the dark troubled corners of the world had come back into the light and there was no more dark or distances at all. A honey-sweet trickle raced from her lips deep into her stomach. She felt her breath rushing against his upper lip. He held her forever. It was like waking from a deep, deep sleep, when daylight came between their faces again. They blinked, amazed at each other, grasping now what had happened. Gabriel's cap wore a tall crown of snow. Géline's dark hair was once again dressed in white. And all her churning anger had turned into happiness.

"What are you doing here?" she asked at last.

"I was helping with the fire at Normand's," he said.

"I couldn't get to sleep."

They looked at each other, a little bewildered now. A brief moment had moved them into a new landscape.

"They can't see us here," said Gabriel awkwardly.

It would have been easier to look down, but she met his gaze. "I don't care."

"I love you, Géline."

She didn't even blink as snowflakes clung to her lashes.

"What?" She had heard, but wanted those words again.

"I love you."

Through the deep baffle of falling snow, came the distant chiming of the breakfast bell.

"What do you mean?"

Gabriel rolled his eyes. "What do I mean!" He took hold of her arm. "I mean that ... that we belong. Just like angels. But for real."

Her eyes were wide and shining now. "I love you too."

Gabriel gave a nervous chuckle. "I hear the boys bragging," he said. "You know, about speedy Suzie, or all the things they get to do with Isabelle ... and I don't care. It's not for real. Not like you."

She brought her hand to his face. "With you I have nothing to hide from God," she said very softly, almost softer than the falling snow.

"Even when we touch?"

She nooded. "Even when we kiss!"

"Even if...?" He caught himself.

Her smile faded. She nodded solemnly. The bell was tolling melodiously from home. Gabriel squinted up into the blinding fall of snow.

"It's not so cold now."

"No," she said. "It's fine." She stuck her tongue out and caught several flakes that melted quickly. "Look!"

Gabriel looked over as she held out her tongue.

"See?" she said after they melted. "Pretty, aren't they? So pretty. But only for a moment and then lost."

"Not lost, just changed...."

"Lost!" She stared grimly into the white glare above.

"You sound angry."

"I am. I'm a snowflake. I'm changing. And I don't want to. Do we have to go way up there to be beautiful?"

"No."

When she looked over, his eyes were full of her.

She peered up into the snowfall. "See how they're twisting."

"Like the inside of my head," he answered. "Géline, listen to me. Some things are not well. We can make them better, you and I. Come with me to Papa."

He offered her his hand. She felt a great joy filling her.

"I'll fight if I have to," he said. "I'll take on both our papas, with one hand behind my back."

Her laugh bounded across the fields. The bell had ceased. They turned and walked hand in hand toward home.

13

AS GABRIEL AND GELINE came up through the orchard, the snow had petered away to nothing. A frail sun touched the weathercock on the barn. The little roof over the well was wearing an oversized helmet of snow. They had decided to see Bénédicte first, since he was on their way. Then they would drag him along to Basile's house. Fat chance, thought Géline, as she held Gabriel's hand up the path to the old willow by Papa's porch. But she had to be brave, now that Gabriel was getting braver. Together they could do better than either of them could do alone.

Gabriel brushed against a loaded branch and a shower of snow sprinkled him from head to toe. Any other time he would have laughed and given her a good branchful too. Now he didn't notice. His face was set on that door. She felt his brave heart through the grip of his hand. From the barn they could hear Charlot loudly cursing the cows for some mid-morning misdemeanour. They looked at each other, but there was nothing more to be said. Géline reached for the latch and opened the door. With her breath held, she stepped into the shadows, pulling Gabriel with her.

The shock was instant. Papa was not alone. And the other voice belonged to Basile Lajeunesse. They stepped into the room to get a full view. There was a fire in the hearth. The elbow-chairs, the spinning wheel, the gleaming tankards on the sideboard, the two papas leaning forward to each other were all dancing in nimble shadows along the timbered wall. Between Bénédicte and Basile was a stool holding their game of checkers. They had heard the latch and were both staring at the door. A long moment lapsed. The clock was clicking. The fire was whispering. Papa's breathing was a little heavy, as so often after breakfast. A long moment took Géline from fear to glorious bravery!

"Good morning, Papa. Gabriel is here with me because he needs to talk to you about me and I ask you to please listen to what he has to say because then it's my turn to say what's in my heart and beg you to...."

"You want to be betrothed to Gabriel, is that it?" spoke Bénédicte.

"I know he's Basile's boy," she pressed on, "but we have a strong affection between us and he'll be a good husband to me."

"That's fine," smiled Bénédicte.

"That's fine, yes, but you don't understand...."

"It's fine."

"You mean.... You mean, it's ... fine?"

"Fine."

"That Gabriel wants me for his wife?"

"That he wants you, yes."

"And that I want him too?"

"Yes, yes, all that," chuckled Bénédicte with his raspy humour.

Géline stared at her Papa, stupefied. She now noticed that he was smiling. And so was Basile, with all of his ample face. And now it sank in, they were playing checkers; as they hadn't done in years. Not since she was twelve or so.

"Have you stopped fighting?" asked Gabriel.

The two papas looked over at each other and there

was magic between them. Géline's chest was heaving with astonishment. She and Gabriel had been poised for a battle.

"We have a lot of work to do, my girl," said Papa. "We must do it together, Basile and I, Philippe and Gérard-in-the-bush, Normand and Denny-on-the ridge, and all the rest. We have to go to Halifax together, all the deputies, to see the new Lieutenant-Governor of Nova Scotia. His name is Lawrence."

They could hear footsteps on the porch outside. Basile and Bénédicte exchanged a glance.

"And to mark the occasion," said Bénédicte, "I, Bénédicte Bellefontaine of Grand-Pré, have given my daughter in betrothal to Gabriel, son of my friend and near neighbour Basile."

Géline's jaw dropped and she was powerless to respond. In her stead, Gabriel stepped forward quickly, kneeled by Bénédicte's chair and embraced him with all his might.

"I thank you, Monsieur. And may the Holy Virgin bless all your days!"

Bénédicte grunted contentedly, patting Gabriel on the back of the head. Géline was dizzy with rapture. As Gabriel rose to thank his papa, she came slowly to Bénédicte and sank with her forehead on his knee. But in her astonishment, she had turned a deaf ear on the approaching footsteps.

Now, as she looked toward the door, her eyes fell on René LeBlanc the notary, smiling impishly as he well knew his errand. She still thought of him as old-man-driftwood, with his shocks of yellow hair like polished floss on a corn cob, hung over his shoulders. Or a labouring oar, bent by the surf of a long life; but not broken. Gabriel hurried to show him a chair by the hearth.

"Good René," said Basile, "sit you down by the fire."

Géline had now recovered sufficiently to fetch the brazen lamp and set it by the notary's chair. He drew from his pocket his papers and inkhorn. Géline was soon filling the pewter tankard with Grand-Pré's nut-brown ale and serving everyone a brimming mug.

"My good children," said René LeBlanc, brandishing his quill above the scroll, "I will tell you something."

Good! she thought. Another of his stories, just like coming home from school.

14

"AND YOU CAN BELIEVE it or not," began René LeBlanc, "but on Christmas Eve when I went up to Normand's stable to hear what the cows were saying, do you know what I heard?"

He looked at Géline quizzically. She squirmed a little.

"Really, Monsieur LeBlanc, cows don't talk."

The notary shook his head. "Oh, Evangéline, don't grow up all at once. On Christmas Eve they do!"

Basile was laughing contentedly behind her. Géline shook her head.

"A cow was talking to her old bull. They were rubbing their heads together and mooing very purposefully. And what do you suppose they were mooing?"

"How should I know?" she shrugged, a little embarrassed.

By now, Papa was in on the fun too. René LeBlanc leaned forward with a conspiratorial air.

"I overheard the cow saying, 'Do you know little Mademoiselle Bijou?' 'Why, certainly!' said the bull." René LeBlanc had altered his voice to suit the more brash persona of the bull, " 'That cute little white one over in Bénédicte's barn.' 'Yes, that's her,' resumed the cow, 'and don't you be making eyes at her either!' "

Now Basile and Bénédicte were having a grown-up chuckle.

" 'She's Evangéline's pet,' continued the cow. 'Well, I was talking to Bijou down by the brook last fall, and she went on and on about her master.' 'You mean

Evangéline?' asks the bull. 'No, that's the master's daughter,' said the cow. 'I mean Bénédicte. Bijou told me how poor little Géline would come to her in the barn to weep her heart out for the love of a young boy.' 'Oh, so he doesn't love her back?' 'Yes, yes, very much,' said the cow. 'Oh, so he's gone away, is that it?' 'No, no, he lives next door,' said the cow. The bull rolled his head side to side. 'So why does Evangéline weep?' 'I'll tell you why,' " continued René LeBlanc in the more gracious voice of the cow, and then paused to sip his ale.

He peered innocuously around the room through the horn-bowed glasses that teetered on his ruddy nose. There wasn't a sound, save the clicking clock and the hissing hearth. His four listeners were riveted. Basile's and Bénédicte's smiles had slipped slowly off their faces. The notary set down his mug of ale, licking the foam from his bearded lip.

" 'I'll tell you what Bijou said,' continued the cow. 'It's because their papas can't get along.' At this, the old bull burst into a loud, hilarious moo. 'You mean she has to forsake her sweetheart because their papas don't get along?' And to this, of course, the cow had to agree. Whereupon the bull burst into riotous gales of mooing, saying, 'How could anyone be so pigheaded!' But he should have weighed his words, because on the instant a wild racket of squealing burst from the pig pen," and now René LeBlanc sounded like a dozen outraged pigs, " 'You watch what you're saying! It wasn't us, it wasn't us,' squealed all the pigs, until the bull had to apologize before they broke down their pen. 'I'm sorry, good oinkers all,' said the bull. 'I guess I really meant to call them featherbrains.' No sooner had he spoken, than the rafters were alive with wings and all the resident

chickens, pigeons, and swallows swooped down upon
him, beating his brow with their swift wings and cack-
ling ferociously, 'Don't you go blaming us for man's
foolery!' This gave the old bull pause. 'You're right,' he
answered. And as the chickens, pigeons, and swallows
returned to their perches, he pondered their words.
'Don't go naming man's foolery after us. Let him name
himself!' "

As the story came to an end, Basile sat like a man who
wished to speak but had no language. All his thoughts
were congealed into lines on his face, just as the vapors
had frozen in fantastic shapes on the window pane.

"My friend," said Bénédicte at last, "your story is just.

My own reckoning is with God. But today may no shadow fall on this house and hearth!" He put his hand out to Géline who took it, trembling. "This is the day of the marriage contract. We'll build you a house and a barn. All our lads will lend their strength. And after Easter, they'll turn your sods and plant your field—food for a twelvemonth and the barn full of hay."

Now the notary wrote with a steady hand the date and the age of the parties, naming the dower of the bride in flocks of sheep and in cattle. All things proceeded quite orderly and were duly and well completed. Evangéline looked at Gabriel. He was smiling from ear to ear. She went to the sideboard and returned with the pipe and the leather pouch of tobacco for Basile. He took them contentedly and gave her a squeeze around the waist.

"When shall be the betrothal?" asked René LeBlanc.

"May we set the first Friday of the harvest?" suggested Basile.

"So be it," nodded Bénédicte.

Gabriel caught Evangéline's eye. Their hearts touched in solemn ecstasy. The great seal of the law was set like a sun on the margin. René LeBlanc recorded the month of September and the year of 1755.

15

JOSEPHINE HAD A prophetic thumb. It would ache and be miserable all winter long. But when her aches let go, she knew it was almost spring. That year, Joséphine was in the church pew with Basile and Gabriel, two Sundays after Easter, when she leaned over and poked her thumb in Basile's rib.

"It's time to plant," she whispered.

He looked over, eyebrows raised in surprise. Spring is early, he thought. Soon time to get the string beans and the pumpkins started. And he'd best be showing the young lads where the house and barn were to go up.

But there were troubles along the way, not the least of them being the Governor's orders from Halifax. Many a time the deputies would all pile into Normand's ox cart and ride off to Halifax to bargain with Lieutenant-Governor Lawrence. Each time, Basile left François in charge of building, but the trips marred their progress. Travelling the rough road to Chebucto Harbour was wearing on Bénédicte's vigour. They wrote a petition together, setting forth articles which would find favour with all Acadians, and took it to Halifax before midsummer. Papa came back despondent. Lieutenant-Governor Lawrence wouldn't even finish reading it.

Father Félicien did teach the children English words, although he wasn't allowed to. Perhaps it was a good thing; they would find plenty of use for them. In the tranquil air of May, Evangéline sat on the porch with Thérèse, Emilie, Isabelle, and her other friends, distaffs in hand to spin golden flax. The sunsets gilded the valley and all the vanes on their chimneys. In hushed, excited tones they would speak their English words to each other, piecing them together in a groping, giggling conversation. Above their heads, the old willow was bursting with lime green buds. Evangéline and Thérèse wore blue kirtles that year and enjoyed walking about together. Evangéline pretended they were sisters. Emilie had a pretty kirtle too, of dark moss green that made her chestnut hair under the white cap shine. If only she wasn't so thin. It made Evangéline feel protective of her.

As the hot weather came creeping up from the steaming mud flats into the valley, Evangéline would load Bijou with tankards of ale and walk her to the clearing where the young lads were stripping bark off the logs for the cabin. Once again she walked among them, a merry tune on her lips, watching as they tipped the frothy ale over their white teeth. Belching friskily, they revived their old ditty, "*Bless this girl! She's the sunshine of Saint-Eulalie.*" Their voices rang in chorus through the woods. She would linger secretly to watch Gabriel straddle the rising wall, his shoulders bare, as he hoisted a log with Baptiste.

After Papa had finished supper, she would stay indoors at the loom. The noisy shuttle worked long after dark, until Papa went upstairs to bed. She was weaving the linens for her dower, the sheets and bolsters and towels. In her clothespress upstairs was the quilt which Emilie's maman had taught her to make when she turned fourteen. That was when the blood had come to her. It came to her at night, so she had tip-toed down the stairs to sit in Papa's elbow-chair, praying for her wound to go away. Her prayers weren't granted, and Papa just kept on snoring until it got light. But when she heard him shuffling on the stair, she couldn't stay to let him see. Wrapped in her longcoat, she had trundled off through the wet grass to knock on Emilie's door. It was her maman that answered, and Evangéline held out the bloodied front of her night shirt. But Madame Godin had smiled, taking her in her arms.

"I have the same wound," she had said softly, showing Evangéline how to take care of herself, "every time the moon comes around. And Viola and Giselle too, and every woman of Acadie. In this way, God wants to remind us that we're not as stubborn and pigheaded as our husbands."

Evangéline had walked home proudly to make breakfast for Papa. She knew she had Madame Godin to go to. And now their quilt had become the precious dower she would bring to Gabriel in marriage, no less worthy than flocks and herds; proof of her skill as a housewife.

"What if Father Le Loutre is really Glooscap?" she said one night, as she worked the loom.

Bénédicte looked up from his cold cider.

"Remember what you told me?" she continued. "What Chief Ulgimoo said? One day Glooscap would return to save his Mi'kmaq people."

Papa gazed out of the window, where Blomidon's ageless profile was blurring in the dusk.

"What are you dreaming about now?" he said softly, a twinkle in his eye.

"I'm not dreaming, Papa. But Lieutenant-Governor Lawrence is driving you too hard. When Father Le Loutre came to us last winter I was afraid of dying, it's true, but his words were good. He cared very much. What if he's Glooscap?"

Papa sat silent. Their rooster was crowing his curfew in the barnyard. "You imagine too much. Don't forget to grow up. You'll be a bride next week." He knocked the tobacco from his pipe. "And the deputies go to Halifax again tomorrow. Maybe I'll stay home."

She gazed at him, his knobbly fingers clasping the cider mug. He made her hurt inside. Papa was so tired, it was as if he had begun to shrink. His shoulder seemed closer to his ear.

"Dear Papa, the old stories are meant to teach us. They can help us to know what we must do today."

"That may be so, my girl," he sighed, "but there's a difference between Glooscap and those who may fancy themselves as Glooscap. A very big difference. And dangerous to everyone!"

The room fell silent. A gentle breeze wafted the cool smell of the mud flats through the room. Evangéline discovered her right hand, still poised on the shuttle. And the clock ticking.

"My dear Papa," she said.

Nothing more. He squinted at her. His smile was dredged from deep despair. And her shuttle slammed, again and again, busily into the night. She would be a bride next week.

16

DENNY-ON-THE-RIDGE brought his sister Marie from
Ile Royale. Basile's cousin, Maurice from Upper Dyke,
came back from Beauséjour. And of course, Gaston
came up from Port Royal! He was Evangéline's older
brother, ten years older, and could remember Maman
very well. He had never been the marrying type and all
Papa's none-too-subtle coaxing couldn't make Gaston
relinquish his own ways and his solitude. He was a
fisherman, and a good one too.

But the deputies did not come. Instead, a ship from
Governor Shirley in Massachusetts had sailed into the
bay of Minas and dropped anchor off Grand-Pré. A
messenger had landed to say that Gérard-in-the-bush,
Philippe, Normand, Bernard-around-the-bend and all
the rest were detained in Halifax, locked in His Majesty's
dungeon on account of what the Governor termed their
ornery natures. The Governor would be calling another
summons at the church in Grand-Pré, and expected all
Acadian menfolk in attendance. Thus read the order
and it was posted for all to see.

But today from all around, from Melanson and
Gaspereau and Canard, the blithe Acadian neighbours
came in their holiday dresses. Many a glad greeting and
giddy giggle made the bright air sparkle. Up from the
pathless meadows came a steady stream of familiar
faces. The village street was thronged with visitors.
Every house was an inn where people sat outside in the
cheerful sun, rejoicing and gossiping.

Under the open sky, in Bénédicte's fragrant orchard, was spread the feast of betrothal. Evangéline and Joséphine had help from Thérèse and Emilie and their mamans in preparing lamb roasts to fill a long table. And all the guests had brought their own specialty. Philippe's Giselle showed up, in his absence, with pans of baked squash. Maurice's Simone brought candied carrots and casseroled green beans. Gaston unveiled his halibut steak seasoned with saffron. All had brought their own best bread. There was cheese bread, molasses bread, bread with dried fruits. And for treats, Yvette Cormier brought Evangéline's favourite—eggs whipped with candied citron peel! All these aromas melded with the tangy breath of the orchard to rouse the palate of one and all.

In the shade of the porch sat Father Félicien and René LeBlanc. The old notary had a child on each knee and many more round about him, listening with wide-eyed wonder to his tales about the Loup-garou in the forest. Bénédicte hobbled up and down the path, welcoming the guests to his home. A short way down the slope, by the ciderpress and the beehives, Michel Gauthier's fiddle was challenging the summer songbirds, luring young and old to kick up their heels in a dance. His wooden shoe beat the time to the music, while the wheels whirled under the orchard trees and down the path to the dykes.

"Two days now, that ship has been at anchor," grumbled Basile. "Look at all their cannons, pointed against us."

He was peering between the apple trees, to the spot where the English ship topped the silvery waves, her sails tucked neatly to the spars.

"Surely some harmless purpose brings them here," said Bénédicte, dipping into his plateful of Gaston's halibut. "Our prosperity is well known. Just weeks ago, we loaded three ox carts to feed the garrison at Fort Piziquid. If the harvest in New England has been blighted by rains, they'll want to stock their ship from our barns and go home."

But Basile was shaking his head. "Don't forget Beauséjour! The Boston mercenaries were ruthless. My cousin will tell you how much French blood was shed on that day!" He pointed to Maurice, who was helping his wife serve the carrots and beans.

"But, they had a special mission to stop Abbé Le Loutre," countered Bénédicte. "Here, they have no enemy."

"We're all commanded to meet in the church," insisted the blacksmith. "Many of our own have crawled like dying dogs into the forest, afraid of tomorrow."

"Has it come to that?" answered Bénédicte. "And with Giselle's husband in jail, and yours too, Yvette— who among us can feel safe?"

"It's a blessing then," prompted Father Félicien, "to see you speaking together instead of fighting."

Basile and Bénédicte looked mischievously at one another.

"Fighting?" said Basile with mock innocence.

"You do us great wrong, Father," said Bénédicte with a semblance of outrage. "I was always comfortable around the likes of Basile. He was always one to see justice done. Fair and square."

Basile grabbed Bénédicte by the shoulder, feeding the bewilderment of their guests. "And when Geline's maman left us, Lord rest her soul," he said, crossing himself, "I thought, *mon Dieu*, who will carry on? But Bénédicte never missed a day. And he raised a daughter who's mannered like a queen."

Bénédicte poked Basile in the ribs. "And will Joséphine say so?"

"She will!" came Joséphine's sharp reply, her face smiling in the crowd beside Evangéline.

"I thank you, honest madame," said Bénédicte, toasting her with his tankard of ale. He stepped in close beside Basile, addressing the merry crowd again. "And here's a man most excellent in his trade."

"Bénédicte's a fellow will talk straight to your face," replied Basile, growing vaguely inspired. "He never made any bones of who he likes and who he doesn't."

"And no more ale for those two!" came Joséphine's crisp dictate.

Laughter rippled softly among the joyous congregation.

Evangéline took Gabriel's hand. "Speaking of mercenaries," she said, her cheek on his shoulder, "do you remember when we were little and you scolded me for swearing?"

He laughed and planted a kiss on her forehead.

"And I had to tell you the meaning of mercenary?" she went on.

"Yes, yes," he sighed, "do you need to rub it in?"

"Too bad, Gabriel, but you're the biggest mercenary that ever was!"

He burst out laughing and grabbed her arm. "By the mother Mary, are you going to stop!"

"You became a mercenary when you first came to my house."

He stared at her in disbelief. "Are you a little drunk, Evangéline?"

She laughed and laid her arms around him. They were behind the willow, so she felt safe.

"It's when you do something for coins even if you don't like it, right?" she whispered to his ear.

"Right."

"And when you came to our house, half asleep and your teeth rattling, to give Papa good luck for the New Year, you just wanted to run home and crawl under the blankets, didn't you?"

Gabriel took a moment to recall that distant morning. "I did, yes."

"But Papa promised you peanuts and a coin, so you came," she said, looking into his eyes beguilingly.

"I did, yes."

She clapped her hands together victoriously. "See! You did it for a coin, even if you didn't like it."

Gabriel grew serious, as he pondered her words. But a new thought smoothed the wrinkle from his brow. "I'll give him back his coin, as long as I can keep you."

Their eyes touched without speaking. She loved him more than words could tell. More than the orchard and Bijou and the old willow put together. It was a searing happiness. She slipped her hand into the dark curls behind his ear and brought his face to hers. When their lips met, there was no strain or confusion. Their kiss was calm and clear as the sky, and as ripe as the cider on their lips. His arms drew her body against him and swung her slowly once around. Then his feet started up with Michel's fiddle and they raced over the grass to join the wheels of the untiring dancers.

That would have been enough in a day. The feast of

betrothal had made it a day to remember. The rekindled friendship between the two papas was cause to celebrate. The imprisoned deputies waiting in the dark somewhere in Halifax gave everyone pause to pray. But it wasn't enough. Now came the church bell, oozing through the orchard with the summons. Evangéline held her breath, thinking for a shining moment that she was hearing her wedding bells. But then she heard, mingled with it, the crisp, brazen roll of the drums.

17

THERESE HAD HER HAND over her mouth. They were all peering up the road. The men's backs were turned, two hundred or more, as they all plodded up the ridge to church. Only the women stayed, strewn like ghosts among the apple trees. A light breeze toyed with a corner of the white tablecloth. A bumblebee, clumsy from cider, had discovered Yvette's eggs with the citron peel. The bell wouldn't stop ringing. Thérèse's hand was still on her mouth.

Why? thought Evangéline, leaning against the willow tree with her arms tucked behind her. Did Thérèse know something? Did they all know?

Slowly, the cider's bubble was bursting inside her, leaving her with shivers. She could see Gabriel walking with Baptiste and Alphonse. Just walking, with hardly a look at each other. Just the random tramp of boots in the dirt and on the grass beside the road, reaching the ridge and vanishing softly into silence. All their shoulders in frayed wool, bobbing slowly over the crest and out of view. Basile and Bénédicte were among the last to disappear. The blacksmith was holding Papa's arm. The papas and boys of Acadie, walking to the orders of King George.

Suddenly, Emilie was at her side. She hooked her arm with Evangéline's. "I saw you dancing with Gabriel," she said, blushing.

Evangéline nodded, but a shadow had come over her. They gazed all around, at the tables, the servings half eaten or just begun, the brimming mugs set aside for a quick whirl in the dance, Michel's fiddle perched on the stoop. It was as if a morning of June, all music and sunshine, could suddenly pause in the sky, and then turn back into the chill of winter. Evangéline was thankful to be interrupted.

"Well, what are we waiting for?"

Everyone turned to see Joséphine Lajeunesse stationed on the porch, hands on her hips.

"Let's get cleaned up. Don't I know my Basile! He won't let those redcoats waste too many words when he could be dancing."

Giselle laughed brightly through her buck teeth.

"You're right," said Yvette. "We might as well be busy until they come home."

Evangéline took Emilie's arm and they walked up to fill the buckets at the well.

Holy Lord our Savior, let the kingdom come in Your name. Give each new day Your blessing and food for our table. Forgive us when we've failed You as we too shall pardon everyone who means us harm or woe. And keep us, O Lord, together, now and evermore. Amen. When Evangéline looked up from her prayer, the sun was touching the weathercock on the barn. Still no sign of Papa.

Across the flattened grass where dancers had twirled, the shadows of familiar things—the barn, the shed, the well, and the orchard—lengthened toward the shore. Evangéline was hunched on the edge of the porch, her knees together, her hands folded on her lap. Emilie had gone home with her maman. Yvette had lugged her bowls and spoons up the orchard to Normand's house. Joséphine marched homeward with Simone to prepare lodgings for her and Maurice. Thérèse and Evangéline shared a warm hug before she followed her maman up to the road. Denny's sister Marie wanted to visit their aunt across the Perreau river. And so forth. Until no one was left. Only Evangéline.

And now the cows, ambling into the barnyard quite forlorn because Charlot wasn't there to hiss at them. Evangéline grabbed a discarded plate of vegetables from the porch and stepped into the yard. Little white Bijou was quick to come running, thrusting her wide nostrils every which way in the crisp autumn air. Good thing she wasn't wearing the bell this year, or she would've made a frightful racket. As Evangéline held out the plate, Bijou's prickly tongue curled around her wrist. She bit her lip, giggling softly. All around, the air had filled with a dreamy, magical light and the landscape lay as if newly created, nestled in the fond lap of autumn. All sounds were attuned. The whir of wings in the drowsy air and the cooing of pigeons, low as murmurs of love. Already the orchard was dotted with dew, as the slanting sun touched a spark to branches hung with russet, scarlet, and gold.

Evangéline played with Bijou's ear, then turned back to the house. She pulled some logs for the hearth and plugged in between them with bark and straw. The elbow-chair would get nice and warm for Papa. Then she climbed the oak stairs to the landing and found some bed linens for Gaston. She paused in her doorway and went to the little window. Stooping down, she peered between the white curtains. The evening star was in the sky, clear and luminous as always at the harvest. She could see the road winding over the ridge, but not a soul stirring. Awash with anxiety, she hurried down the stairs and spread the straw mattress for Gaston. She laid the table with a fresh cloth and set her brother's and her papa's place, each with a tankard of ale and a loaf of bread with cheese. The fire was crackling and her cheeks tingled with the heat. She placed forks beside the plates and looked around. Shadows danced their ghostly jig along the wall; idle shadows of empty chairs. The clock's constant ticking. Through the window, the grass was sinking to grey. With a gasp, she dropped the knives on the tablecloth and ran for the door.

Evangéline ran blindly until she got to Baptiste's house. There were no lamps lighted at the notary's. In the bluish dusk, she couldn't make out the woman who was approaching from the village with a rapid, weaving sort of walk. As she got closer, the soft moonlight revealed Madame Giselle's features, drawn into a pallid mask of tears.

"Good evening," spoke Evangéline, and reached out for the woman's hand.

But Giselle stared at her like a stranger, her eyes gouged with weeping, and shook her head slowly with lips tightly sealed.

"Where have you been?" stammered Evangéline.

But it was certain that Giselle hadn't heard. Her ears were ringing with something other. Still shaking her head, the poor woman shuffled on towards Basile's house, her hand groping as if to find support in the air. Evangéline walked along the village street, her limbs heavy with a sudden dread. She had to force every breath, although she had walked twice as far all summer long.

At last the church came into view. It was quite dark by now, but she couldn't miss the tents. Beside the church and across the village green, dingy canvas tents billowed in the breeze. Behind them, orderly rows of cavalry horses were crunching contentedly on Grand-Pré oats. A low palisade enclosed the tents and reached to the church presbytery. Evangéline stood very still. The evening star gleamed dispassionately. She folded her arms against the soft chill of night. With her knees knocking, she ventured closer. The English soldiers moved casually among their tents, chatting sparsely with each other. In front of the church door, two armed redcoats were stationed with bayonets mounted. Evangéline peered all around for a sign of someone she knew. At length, she walked into the circle of the English torches. One of the soldiers was eyeing her, without moving. She paused. He wasn't pointing his gun. She came closer. The torchlight flickered eerily across the timbers of the church. The windows were dark and the great oak door barred. She touched her skirt in a cautious curtsey.

"*Salut*," she said, choking on that single word.

The soldier's gaze was unchanged. She felt a need to sit down. With a silent blessing to Father Félicien, she mustered her English words.

"Can Gabriel … come?"

The soldier was unimpressed.

"Can Gabriel come?" she repeated.

The soldier shook his head slowly from side to side. A sudden ache flared up in her chest. She stepped toward him. With a quick metallic snap, the musket came between them. She stood for a moment, breathing deeply.

"I am … Gabriel's … wife," she said.

The soldier looked over at his comrade, who made

some sort of exasperated face. They shrugged their shoulders.

"Go home," said the other soldier without coming closer.

That much she could understand.

"Go home now," he repeated, still not budging from his post.

The evening star had faded, as the moon rose in a mist over the marshes. Evangéline followed the moonlight with her eye. Ripples on the water, silver drowning in pitch. Her eye was steady and clear. The dark masts hiding in the silvery bay. The soldiers' ship. *Horses don't sail*. Where had all the horses come from?

"Hey, you."

Evangéline looked back at the soldier.

"Go home," he said. And then, in a lower voice, "Pack your things."

She was proud that she recognized the English words.

"Pack all that you want to remove from your home."

18

THE COWS WERE IN AGONY. They yielded their bloated udders blissfully to Evangéline as she filled the pails one by one, up and down the stable. It was a sin to keep Charlot from his work! Had they no feelings, locking a man inside the church when he had work to do! Poor cows! Old Lou-lou stood bleary-eyed, legs wide apart, as the milk sprayed rhythmically into the wooden pail. The rooster crowed brightly next door and Evangéline knew it was near dawn. She was ready for sleep, but there would be no rest. She emptied all the pails into Papa's dairy trough. Then she pushed the great barn door open and shooed the cows off to pasture. Light and lively, they pranced into the morning mist. Bijou was butting one of her friends in the ribs.

Evangéline leaned on the doorpost, gazing after the carefree herd. *Pack your things.* Those were his words. *All that you want to remove from your home.* She had walked straight home, then up through the orchard to Normand's. There were lights in the window. Yvette had opened her arms to Evangéline and they had cried together. Yvette had heard it all from Joséphine and was already packing. When Evangéline got back to Papa's house, Joséphine had been waiting in front of the fire.

"Devils," she growled. "Miserable little devils!"

So they packed half the night, before Joséphine would go home. And now the cock was crowing. Evangéline sat at the table, tasting her bread with eggs and honey. She pressed her eyes shut to stop the tears that made dark spots on her bread. At least this way she would soon see Papa and Gabriel. On the hearth, the fire was still smouldering. A great stillness lay everywhere. The leaves of the willow rustled against the window. There was nothing gloomy or evil, just a deep stillness. She listened. Once again, the clock's ticking was hiding from her. She held her breath. The ticking was not there. It really wasn't there. She looked over into the dusky corner. The hands showed one hour past midnight. The clock had stopped. The room was still. She couldn't move. The house had stopped. The sun was rising but her house had stopped.

Wagon wheels on the road. Grinding. Evangéline jumped. She looked out of the window and saw Emilie walking beside the hay wain, and Madame Godin driving the oxen toward the village. A lot of time must have passed. Evangéline bounced from her seat. With frantic fingers she pried open the clock's wooden belly and set it against the wall. She reached in and unhooked the leaden weights, the way she'd seen Papa do it, and laid them side by side. Then she wound the two chains back up and set the hands at seven hours. That wouldn't be too far off. Gently, she hung the weights and fitted the front panel into its groove. Anyway, Papa would know the correct time. She put out the last embers of the fire. That was important, even just to go to market. Some of her skirts and stockings and linens were piled on a sheet by the door. She gathered the corners of the sheet and slung it onto her back. As she gazed around the room, her head was reeling. It was empty. A timbered cell, stark floors to stark ceiling. A few odd scraps. The spinning wheel was broken anyway. Papa would've tried to mend it, but never mind. Only the table by the window. With a start she ran to the table and pulled out the little drawer. She lifted a wooden box with Papa's checkers and tucked it into the bundle on her back. She closed the drawer neatly and paused for a moment. The willow whispered at the window.

"Maman," she said.

The clock was her only answer. She peered up to the oak rafters. "Maman, I have to go."

Her knuckles on the sheet were white. "Papa needs me. I'll put everything back when we get home."

She reached overhead and touched her hand to the rough-hewn wood. As the door shut behind her, she pushed the bolt as far as it would go.

Over the yellow fields came a village on wheels. The women perched on rickety, broad-wheeled wains with their household goods packed for the high road. Thérèse was walking next to her maman's wain, holding little Hugo by one hand while his other hand clasped a bark sailboat. On the ridge, she turned to see her bedroom window before it was shut from her sight by the winding road.

"Thérèse!"

It was Evangéline, driving her papa's wain up from the barnyard.

"*Salut!*" answered Madame Viola.

"Did you do it all by yourself?" asked Thérèse.

"No, never!" called Evangéline. "Joséphine was over. And she helped me hitch the oxen too."

"She's right behind us," said Madame Viola.

And sure enough, there was the blacksmith's wagon, loaded to the rim and Joséphine presiding, while talking under her breath to the old ox. Her eyes were drawn to dark slits, her lips pursed in defiance. There could be no doubt that the ox was hearing some choice language!

"Bravo, *p'tite* Géline!" she called.

Evangéline waved fondly. Thus, to the church they drove their caravan of chattels.

They were getting down from the wagons when the great church doors opened. Everyone looked up. The children's frisky voices fell silent. From the darkness of the church came the English guards, marching slowly with muskets at their shoulders. After a moment, Evangéline noticed the bare-headed one. His jacket had a rip at the shoulder and there was a dark swelling below his eye. But he marched with the rest, his gaze fixed in front of him. Her heart started pounding as she scanned the others. But no one else showed any sign of upset. The soldiers started downhill toward the shore.

"Papa!" blurted little Hugo and ran toward the church.

There, in the doorway, stood Henri Benoît. But a soldier stepped quickly in front of the racing boy and Viola yelled, "Stop, Hugo, stop it! Get back here!"

Hugo ground to a halt, squinting up at the soldier. Thérèse caught up with him, while new faces emerged from the dark. René LeBlanc stepped gingerly over the threshold. There was Alphonse, a ghostly white, his eyes darting anxiously. And old Charlot, staring down at his boots. Denny-on-the-ridge, puffing endless air through clenched teeth. Their eyes were dull. Some shirts were torn. Emilie's papa searched the crowd for his family. Baptiste emerged with sad, hangdog eyes— but separated from his Papa René, thought Géline with puzzlement—and behind him, Gabriel! He was helping Basile, whose head was bandaged with somebody's shirt. The cloth was dark with blood. His left eye was only a slit in a bulging black bruise. Although he had his arm over Gabriel's shoulder, he was limping badly. Evangéline's head was swimming. They had hurt him. Somebody had beaten Basile blacksmith. Other faces followed, stepping unsteadily into the glaring day. One or two bore the scars of a scuffle, the rest were simply vacant, sullen, vanquished.

Papa! No one was helping him through the door. But he had no bruises! He looked fine! She ran toward him and discovered Joséphine racing at her side. Two of the rear guards stepped into their path with bayonets at the ready.

"Now listen to me," snarled Joséphine, pointing toward Basile. Her finger was trembling. "That's my Basile. That's what you've done to my Basile!"

She walked straight for the bayonets as they lowered to meet her. A whinnying of horses made her halt. Up on the grass embankment, where Father Félicien liked to teach, came half a dozen uniformed horsemen. They reined in their horses at some distance to observe the scene. In their midst, Evangéline saw a haunted face, the front rider of her childhood memory. Once again he sat before her, mechanically sliding his hand along the horse's muscular neck. She was dazed. She had always thought evil would wear an ugly face, as in Father Félicien's books. The Antichrist. Swollen with savage pleasures. Hideously bloated with unnatural thoughts. Haggard from unnameable acts. But this was no such face. If she had met him anywhere else, she might have thought him handsome. And no bigger than Papa! There was nothing wicked in his appearance. Instead, he showed deep fatigue, a profound collapse of spirit behind a mask of stoic endurance.

"Colonel Winslow, sir," said Joséphine, "my husband has been hurt."

The front rider looked from Basile to Joséphine. He gave a nod to the guards, who withdrew their bayonets. Evangéline rushed forward.

"You're not hurt!" she sobbed and held Papa tenderly.

But his eyes told her otherwise. From behind, she felt Gabriel's warm hand enfolding hers, and their eyes met with wonder and pain. The procession continued slowly down the hill, as Joséphine ripped her skirt into clean strips for Basile's head. She was talking to him under her breath, as she had talked to her old ox. Their shoulders touched. But no one else was allowed forward. The bayonets stopped Emilie and her maman and everyone else trying to get close.

"Your men are prisoners by His Majesty's orders," commanded the colonel loudly. "Be patient. You may mingle in the boats."

Thus saying, he touched his heels to the horse and started downhill alongside the Acadians, his men riding after.

Evangéline thought Basile was whispering to Joséphine, but then she saw his half-turned face, battered and grisly, and knew it was to her. She leaned closer.

"Yes?"

"The aboiteaux, Géline. Open the floodgates."

But the tide is in! She stared at him. He smiled through his bruises. She looked over at Papa. He gave a slow nod.

"You can do it, my girl," he said. "Take your friends. All seven aboiteaux. Drown Acadie."

She looked to the north. From where they were, it was the same view she'd had every morning in springtime, where Father Félicien's droning syllables would mingle with the chickadees and woodpeckers. She could count the seven aboiteaux, their floodgates shut against the tide to protect the golden wheat, the silk-plumed corn, and the flax. This was the treasury of Grand-Pré, the winter's hope, swaying like a singing sea in the wind. *Drown Acadie*. Her hand grasped Gabriel's.

"Be of good cheer," he said. "While we love each other, nothing can come between us."

His hand slipped away with Basile. Her hand stayed behind. She gazed after them. Gabriel was smiling impishly over his shoulder. She'd do it for his smile. Drown Acadie!

19

THE TIDE WAS ALREADY TURNING. Dragging its quarrelsome pebbles back into the sea, the tide had left the English rowboats stranded for the day. But now the water was on its way back.

"We don't have much time," whispered Evangéline.

She ran, half-stooped, through the tall wheat inside the dyke. Charging behind her came Thérèse, Emilie, and Isabelle. The four of them should manage. It was the strangest thing she'd ever done, running to the aboiteaux with Papa's blessing! Opening the floodgates out of season. To drown the crop. And, as if she had no shame, her fingers were itching to do it!

"What if they kill us?" whispered Isabelle.

"They can't see this far down the shore," said Thérèse, panting.

"But from the ship!" hissed Isabelle.

Maybe she shouldn't have come, thought Evangéline. "We'll have to work fast," she said aloud. "If they

discover us, they'll get here in ten minutes. We've got to reach all seven aboiteaux before they can stop us."

That shut Isabelle up. It was twilight, so visibility from the ship would be reduced.

If only Gabriel could be here. And Baptiste and Alphonse! Like the old days. The forbidden forest. The big capture. The boys would've loved this one. Gabriel had to be kicking himself! The greatest ambush of all time.

This time it was different. It wasn't just for themselves. Papa was on their side. And so were they all. Back at the campfires on the beach, the word would spread in whispers and glances. All of Grand-Pré was behind them. Papa's grave old eyes were betting on his little tadpole. Everyone was waiting. Listening in the twilight. Wondering. *Is it done? Is it done?* Evangéline spat at some chaff that had stuck on her face, and they scampered through cattails and bullrushes into the clear and up the side of the dyke. Beside them was the dark timber of the aboiteaux.

"Did you really hear your papa say yes?" crooned Emilie.

"Yes, yes, I did," hissed Evangéline. "And Papa Basile too."

They peered carefully over the top. On the bay, the English ship was serene and immobile. Ready for the morrow. Evangéline quickly sized up the task.

"Isabelle, can you stay here with Thérèse? Emilie will come with me to the other side."

The girls nodded, now infected with excitement. Thérèse and Isabelle clambered down beside the damp timbers of the floodgate. Evangéline held Emilie's hand across the aboiteaux. Emilie's hand was shaking like a captive bird. "To this point but no farther," recalled Evangéline with a shudder of delight. They slid down to the muddy channel and Evangéline raised her hand for ready. The others answered. They held the bar that would pin the gates open.

"We have to be strong," said Evangéline in a half-whisper, and her voice was trembling. *Death to the mercenaries!*"

They all took a good hold on the wood, counted to three, and gave a mighty heave together. It was easy. Before they knew it, they were looking through to the ocean. The tide was their ally; it would not stop at the door.

On the shore, the evening fires had been kindled. They had scavenged for driftwood beached by storms from the open Atlantic. Piled in confusion between the fires lay the household goods of each family. Like a gypsy camp, guarded by the water's edge and on the other side by Colonel Winslow's men, the Acadians huddled close to the sputtering heat. Bénédicte had spread his blanket near the mouth of the Gaspereau, and was peering across the fire into the dark. His features were watchful, wary, anxious. It was getting late. Doubts were nagging him. At the neighboring fire, Yvette and Alphonse had settled in for the night, along with Giselle. Farther up the beach, Bénédicte could see Viola Benoît tucking in her little Hugo. Henri was at her side, but no sign of Thérèse. He peered over at the bundled bulk beside him, from which protruded Gaston's tousled hair. Lucky boy, thought Bénédicte. He had somehow put the day far enough from his thoughts to get some sleep. Gaston was a strange bird for keeping his own pace. Over on the rear edge of the camp, Father Félicien could be seen waddling from fire to fire, as he had from home to home in the parish. Directly beyond the good Father's head, Bénédicte sighted the vague mass of his house flanked by the willow tree. There was no moon tonight. The dark was endless.

He flinched as a shadow emerged from the bushes. It was Géline, blessed be Mary! He held his arm out to her and she walked barefoot into the fire's glow, taking his hand between hers.

"Where is Thérèse?" he asked hoarsely.

"With Viola and Henri," she answered.

"And what about Emilie and Isabelle?"

"Each with their mamans."

"So what about...?"

In Papa's eye was the final, looming question. There was no mistaking her smile. His hand grasped hers.

"Yes, Papa, it is done."

He drew her close and hugged her to his chest. "All seven?"

"All seven."

"I knew it, *p'tite* Géline," he said, puffing a contented chuckle through his cheeks. He held her at arm's length and their eyes met. "I don't have my tadpole any more."

Squeezing her hand, he began to sing.

"Holy Father, let the kingdom
Come in Your name.
Give each new day Your blessing
And food for our table...."

Evangéline was a little embarrassed. It wasn't like Papa to grow sentimental, especially in the hour of distress. Perhaps at home around the hearth, eating and toasting in the merry company of friends, yes, perhaps then. But not here. Not now! She felt her cheeks flush.

"Papa," she urged anxiously.

But his eyes smiled at her while his raspy voice lifted the hymn into the night. And as she peeked around, she could see no one looking to ask what was the matter with Papa. Instead, others were joining in. More voices, up and down the beach. As she gazed in wonder, the singing spread like a bushfire from family to family, fire to fire, right under the noses of the guarding redcoats. It was like magic. The whole beach was singing.

"Forgive us when we've failed You
As we must pardon too
Everyone who means us harm or woe.
And keep us, O Lord, together,
Together."

Papa stopped singing, while the hymn repeated itself again and again, rising on the smoke from their fires.

"Why is everybody singing?" she stammered.

"Because everybody knows," he said.

"What, Papa?"

"What you've done."

She was stunned. As the truth dawned on her, tears blurred everything from her sight. It was not a song of sadness. It was victory. Right under the noses of the English. And the soldiers wouldn't know until morning. She wiped her eyes and waved over to Yvette's fire. Thérèse was waving back. Now they were sisters! Overcome, she squatted by the flames to dry her soaking skirt. She let her fingers pinch a tempting tuft of Gaston's hair and gave it a yank. Not even a twitch disturbed his slumber.

"Where is Gabriel?" she asked suddenly.

Papa frowned. "He went off to argue with the officers. They took Basile and Joséphine already."

Evangéline looked up.

"After what happened in church, they didn't want Basile talking with the rest of us. So they shoved him into one of their boats. But Joséphine put one foot in the boat and said, 'If you take him, you better take me too.' Well, bless her heart, they had enough sense to know what they were up against! So, in she went and now they're on the ship. And Gabriel is fuming."

"Are we all going?" she whispered at length.

Papa couldn't look at her. "They're expecting more ships."

20

"WHAT DID BASILE DO?" asked Evangéline.

Bénédicte made a gesture of futility, squinting into the smoke.

"What he did?" smiled Papa fondly. "He was Basile, that's what he did!" And after a moment's contemplation, "That's all he did. You see, they had a small table in the aisle. They had stripped the church to nothing. The cloths and the candles and even the Christ—everything was gone. 'I have received the King's instructions,' said the Colonel. He was sitting at the table, you understand, unfolding his piece of paper. And we stood packed like shamefaced schoolboys. In our own church. Weren't those his words, Father?"

Father Félicien was finally getting around to them, approaching at a steady waddle. He had not been singing with the rest.

"Tell her the King's orders," said Papa.

Félicien met Evangéline's gaze with a wan smile. "Our lands and tenements and cattle and livestock. That's how it begins. All forfeited to the Crown of England, except money and household goods."

"Bijou!" gasped Evangéline. "*Mon Dieu!*"

She would have jumped to her feet, but Papa caught her by the wrist.

"All French inhabitants are to be removed from this colony," continued the Father softly.

"Yes, even so. That's what he said," growled Papa. "Straight to our faces. It drove Basile mad."

"In the house of God," spoke Father Félicien. "Did Basile think because the crucifix was gone, that Christ was no longer there?"

Papa glowered in Félicien's direction, but went on. "Basile took hold of the nearest guard and flung him clear to the door. But there were too many, like wolves on the shanks of a moose, clubbing him down with their muskets. He might as well have been a bull for the slaughter."

Evangéline felt the air bristle between Papa and Father Félicien.

"Don't you hear the words?" said the Father, with his little peppercorn eyes on Papa. "Listen to their singing: *'Pardon too / Everyone who means us harm or woe.'* You sang it first. You sing and know not what you sing! Twenty years have I spent among you. Is this the fruit of my labours? Have you forgotten all lessons of love and forgiveness? To turn our church into a battleground! Where is meekness and holy compassion? Where speaks the crucified Christ: 'Father, forgive them'?"

Not until he had paused, could Evangéline start breathing again. Papa met his gaze with something worse than disappointment. She wanted to understand but, at that moment, the sky changed. The many-throated singing stopped all at once. It was the sky. Men, women, and children peered up the hill. From the south rose a ghostly, unnatural dawn, usurping the night with shooting fingers, gleaming through the black brushwood, glowing farther and farther across land and sea. The hush slowly shaped a dreadful sound. It was a low hum, and as they listened closely it became an incessant crackling and breaking of wood, melding to a mighty, droning roar. Columns of smoke billowed over the trees, dwarfing their own little fires, as if Glooscap and all the heathen gods had made their own camp just up from the Acadians. Cinders and flashing flames kept darting into the darkness. A death-like stillness had settled upon everyone. As the wind picked up, large sheets of burning thatch drifted and scattered in the air.

Somewhere at the back of her head, Evangéline heard a low, tremulous sobbing and slowly realized it was her own. From the hundred housetops of Grand-Pré sprung the quickening smoke, riddled with ashes and flame. And all across the beach burst the dykes of human endurance, welling forth from Acadian hearts in howls of pain and long, shuddering wails of despair. As if to answer them one last time, came from the barns the eerie, wailing squeal of frenzied animals. Evangéline rose to her feet. The smell of doom was in her nostrils, as on that winter's night when she had looked across the orchard and seen Normand's barn a-torch. Cows, horses, pigs, chickens, all thrashing to break away from the flames. From the folds of his sleep, Gaston appeared at her side, staring with eyes round and glazed, only moments away from comprehending.

"Bijou!" yelled Evangéline, but her voice was lost in the pandemonium of the beach.

She looked over to their orchard. Flame, all flame! The willow tree was a torch against the night.

"Bijou! *Mon Dieu*, and Lou-lou! My Bijou!"

Papa's hand came down on her shoulder. How was it she knew, so surely, that it was for the last time? The hand that had cupped her shoulder riding to Mass, bringing the apple cart up through the orchard, leaving her for the first time to study with Father Félicien. Could this hand, most dear and fundamental to all her years, be a stranger all at once? Why now so brushing and incidental, like a fumble, as in passing? Instinctively her hand went up to clasp his, to hold it there. She turned. His eyes were open wide but he didn't see her nor anything else, and the sky was in his eyes, nothing more. Papa was gone from his eyes! And those eyes, empty mirrors to the flaming sky, fell away from her forever. Fell to the ground.

"Papa," she whispered, "I'll come too. Wait, Papa, I'm coming. I want to come with you." She was screaming now. "I want to come with you! I want to come with you! I want to...."

At last, she plummeted into darkness.

21

WILD GEESE ARE ALWAYS ahead of themselves. They have no need to look down. Wearing the wind, they trust to the stars and the sun's steps on the curvature of the earth. The topography below has no meaning. They are half way to somewhere else. They are reaching for the distance, sweeping down the highroad of heaven, and there's nothing they won't leave behind, except this one thing; their mournful, honking cry.

The geese have no need to look down. With their necks stretching for tomorrow, they barely flinch at wisps of smoke or other such impurities in their path. Were they creatures of earth instead of air, they might bow their necks long enough to see where the trailing wisps began, knotting into a hundred columns of black, billowing smoke from the little shore of Minas. And those that came after, the last to leave for the south, did not see the blackened, scattered traces of Grand-Pré, almost obliterated by a cover of fresh snow. But geese don't look down. Such is time. And the nature of change. The daily chores make a lot of noise, but the sweep of history is silent as the heart.

And when the seasons had circled once again and the geese came trailing through the leaden air with mournful, honking salute, there was no one on the church step. There was no church step; no church. There was no schoolgirl with brown tresses at her ear, gazing dreamily after the geese. There was no boy peeking over to see her

thin, proud neck and feel happier. It was all ashes, beaten down into the silent soil and blown into the shifty winds. Who was left to speak? No one to say how it had been. The memory was nowhere.

But the geese don't look sideways. They come back and go, come back and go again. Each year something goes with them. As they soar overhead, they pluck the last crumbs of summer from the shores of Acadie. Were they creatures of earth instead of air, they might bow their necks long enough to notice that smoke came from new chimneys, new roofs. That there were new wagons in the barnyard, different words at supper tables, other hymns in a different church, other children with the same laughter. These were the Planters, taking their cue from Governor Shirley in Massachusetts. Prime farmland, theirs for the taking if they would settle Nova Scotia for His Majesty King George.

As they winged across the Atlantic main, the geese veered west. The new coast spread before them. Had they looked down, they would have discovered the timbered clutter of Boston harbor, giving way to broad, rolling woodlands rising through the Catskills and climbing jaggedly into the Appalachian Mountains. Down below their airy world of wings, people were crawling ashore from putrid ships, stretching canvas over bulging ox carts, kicking at the rock that broke their wheel, striking stones together for a spark to start their fire, stepping into army tents to ask about the new trail. The geese swooped down the Delaware, hardly aware of the young town of Philadelphia just before the riverbend. Even if they had looked, they would have seen no trace of the ox carts.

Leaving the coastline and the bustling harbors behind, the geese shot straight for the cold air of the mountains. Up to the lonesome source of the Potomac River and gliding into the warmer welcome of the Ohio Valley. Had they looked down, they would have seen the beaten trail, riddled with wagon tracks, but who is to say which track and how far or how long ago? Besides, Braddock's Gap is nothing but granite. Nobody leaves their mark on granite. And once you're in the Valley, there's no need of wheels. A couple of weeks' work by the river bank and you're ready to launch the flat-bottomed johnnyboat and unload the ox carts for the long ticket south.

But where did they launch? And how far have they come? Geese don't look anyway. They're already half way to the horizon, tracing the silver ribbon of the Ohio. By the stars and by the steps of the sun, they approach the land of their destiny. Passing the swampy mouth of the Wabash, they speed across the golden stream of the broad Mississippi. Had they bowed their necks even once, they would have seen the boat. A mere speck on the mighty water, making good speed downstream. But what's that to a wild goose? The wind is so swift and simple. Before you know it, the flock is swooping for a Louisiana bayou two hundred miles away. The sun is low. The stars take over.

With people it's different. Unless they are angels, as in the hearts of children and the very devout, people have no wings. They go slowly. They poke around in the world and in their memories, certain that some day they'll turn over a stone and the underside will be crawling with reasons. If they don't find that stone, all they can do is forgive. Forgive, but not forget. Never forget.

"How many shovels do you need to bury an Acadian?"

The voice rang clear over the wide water. There was no mistaking Gaston Bellefontaine.

"Shhh!" came the admonishing propriety of Father Félicien.

It was not a small boat. Twenty bodies were huddled together, with their belongings bundled in the prow and in the stern. There were four pairs of oars, but two pairs were tucked away just now because the waters were smooth and easy.

"How many shovels?" insisted Gaston, pulling his oar toward him in time with his mate.

"How many what?" asked Baptiste from the prow.

"How many shovels to bury an Acadian?" called Gaston over his shoulder.

There were little murmurs and wisecracks up and

down the boat. Viola and Yvette had their heads together.

"Tell us, how many?" said Viola at last.

"Nine."

"*Mon Dieu*, why?" asked Alphonse.

"One to bury him and nine to shut him up!"

Gaston smiled from ear to ear. Punchlines were his favorite. Laughter burst from everyone as they felt the punch of the joke, their unspoken bond of common faith and common misfortune.

"That makes ten," burst out Alphonse.

"Ten?" asked Gaston.

"Ten shovels. Not nine," laughed Alphonse. "You've lost count!"

He laughed some more and Gaston realized his error, made a face at Alphonse and mumbled something about little do-good schoolboys.

"Now, now," enjoined Father Félicien gently, "I think everyone's had his say. Perhaps Acadian graves are not happy talk for any of us."

The Father looked reproachfully at Gaston. His priestly words left an awkward silence in the boat. His propriety had an uncanny way of achieving the opposite to what he intended. When he wished to banish memories of death, he managed instead to remind everyone of their despair. Only the gurgling river could be heard, as faces turned sympathetically to Evangéline. Others looked at Baptiste, who had lost his old Papa René on the transport ship. Weakened by three days of sea sickness, the smallpox finally took him. Baptiste had watched when they dropped him overboard. Evangéline really felt for him. Back in the mountains before the river, he had told her how his papa's silk-floss hair was last to go under. She didn't like those thoughts. It took her back to the deep darkness where she had looked for Papa, where she first learned that her life was separate from his. At least Maman now had his company, she reminded herself, gazing over the side of the boat.

Across the waves she could see a silvery sandbar stretching down the channel and, wading along its edge, a large bird with a strange ballooning beak.

"Look!" she cried, pointing.

"Oh, yes," said Alphonse, "it's a…. It's a…."

"Pelicans," said Thérèse.

"Pelicans, yes!" said Evangéline.

"Yes, those are pelicans," said Alphonse authoritatively.

"Thank you, Alphonse," said Thérèse teasing.

She knew how best to deal with him. He grinned contritely and put his arm around her shoulder. They were good together. Evangéline watched them with a little smile. They would be married, for sure.

Pelicans. Strange birds. But very beautiful, she thought to herself. Like everything in this land! Sands like silver. Skies of blue crystal. Groves of orange and citron shining along the shore. A daily parade of startling scents. A nightly stir of mysterious sounds and utterances. Most of what they saw was unknown, as yet without a name. It was a wondrous voyage, tasting the newness of the world with no words to name it.

22

"LONG AGO IN an ancient city, whose very name is lost, a stone statue stood in the public square."

Father Félicien paused to receive the bowl of chowder from Yvette's hand. She and Viola had cooked the trout Gaston had brought them, and now they were lounging on the riverbank at dusk, the cooking fire gone to embers. Behind them was the smooth, grassy plain of Opelousas, purple in the twilight. Unreal. Too lovely not to be a painting. The sun was low. The stars were taking over. Father Félicien grunted contentedly, licking the chowder from his lips. He glanced at the stars.

"Bless this food, O Lord."

Everyone joined in the Amen.

"And a blessing upon your heads, Mesdames Benoît and Cormier, for making miracles with Gaston's catch."

The two women nodded graciously as everyone showed their appreciation with grunts and groans and smacking of the lips.

"I helped too," said Thérèse.

The Father eyed her with mock distrust, until Viola said, "She did. She's a good little cook, if I do say so."

Father Félicien chuckled benignly. Alphonse heaved a sigh of pride. His future was secure.

"But that's the last of the cornmeal," remembered Yvette. "Next farm or trading post, we'd better stock up."

"As I was saying," continued Father Félicien with his

heaped spoon poised in the air, "raised on a column, a statue of Justice stood in the square." Downing his spoonful quickly, he used spoon and bowl as props to illustrate the statue. "In its left hand were the scales of justice. In the right hand, a sword to say that justice ruled the land. But you remember Babylon!"

Evangéline did, because she used to enjoy the stories he told them for catechism class.

"Well, that's what it was like. Even the birds built their nests in those scales, forgetful of the sword pointing blindly above them. And in the course of time, the laws of the land were corrupted. Might took the place of right. The weak were oppressed. The mighty ruled with a rod of iron."

Everyone had settled back on their elbows or stretched out on the ground, and the twilight yawned for a good story.

"Then it chanced in a nobleman's palace that a necklace of pearls was lost. Before long, suspicion fell on the orphan girl who lived as a maid in the household. After a quick trial, she was condemned to die on the scaffold. And die she did, hanged according to law. But even as her innocent spirit ascended to her Father in heaven, lo! Over the city rose a tempest, and bolts of thunder struck the statue of stone. From its left hand, the scales of justice fell to the pavement below. In one of the scales, a magpie had built her nest, and woven in its walls was the necklace of pearls. The stolen pearls!"

Father Félicien scraped the last of the chowder from his bowl. His spoon was the only sound in a great silence. How could this limitless place fit in a single stillness? Not even the birds could speak. Evangéline tipped her head back on Thérèse's kneecap.

"What does it mean?" asked Yvette at length. Tears were in her eyes.

Father Félicien cleared his throat. "It's about God and men," he said. "Man is blind, but God is just. In the end, justice triumphs."

Yvette met his gaze, and her lip was trembling. "In the end, yes. But how long is that? It's over two years ago we left home." She hid her face in her hands.

Evangéline took Yvette in her arms, stroking her gently. "I know," she said. "I know it too. You're waiting to find Normand and I'm waiting for Gabriel. But we don't have to wait forever. We're almost there!"

"It's true, Maman," said Alphonse, his hand on her wet cheek. "We lost half a winter in Philadelphia waiting to get off the ship, and it was spring before we heard tell of the river Teche. But now we know the way. You wait and see!"

Yvette looked at her son. His pale, friendly face. "Yes," she said, nodding wearily. "Yes, I know. But I get tired."

"Bless you, woman of Acadie," whispered Father Félicien, his little peppercorn eyes smiling. "Let our Father give you courage. And His Son on the Cross. To have courage is to trust. Remember, sorrow and silence are strong, and patient endurance is godlike."

She blinked away her tears, and blew her nose for the wide plains to hear. In the gathering dark, Thérèse, Isabelle, Evangéline, and Madame Viola took care of the cleaning up. Alphonse and Papa Henri rounded up some help to load the boat.

23

AT NIGHT, there were alligators. At least, that's what Alphonse said it was, but they hadn't actually seen one. A sudden splash usually followed by a muffled snapping sound. The teeth springing like a trap on a heron or muskrat or other denizen of the marshes. The landscape was changing. The water had lost its blue and was turning a sluggish brown. The flat Opelousas had been obscured by a swamp where cypress and cedar grew to terrifying heights, engulfing the johnnyboat in perpetual shadow. Day or night, a ghostly gloom hung beneath the branches. This was the Bayou Plaquemine, where they were soon lost in a maze of devious waters. Somewhere on the far side was the mouth of the Teche, their journey's goal.

Baptiste gave a shudder. Most of the others were asleep. Alphonse and Henri Benoît were in front of him, at the oars. Slowly, cautiously, they were guiding the sleepers through the night. At the front, Gaston was on his knees among the covered household goods, keeping a lookout. With hands cupped around his mouth, he would let out a single, solitary cry and wait for an answer. No human sound came back. There was much out there, but nothing they wanted to meet. Baptiste shuddered again. The forlorn whoop of a crane answered Gaston's call, echoing and rebounding in the tangled boughs overhead. Flitting timidly above the leafy web, moonlight touched their path with silver, glancing and gleaming on the murky water. Dreamlike and indistinct, it stroked the vaulted boughs of cedar, trailing with vines and creepers and mosses dangling in mid-air like banners on an ancient ruin.

A sense of wonder and foreboding filled Baptiste. His roving eye stopped at Evangéline. She was slumped against an oak chest with her head down, the white cap a little askew, dark tendrils curling over her folded neck. Thin like her papa's. But so proud. Just like his ... had been. He sighed deeply. Just to look at her made every place like home.

"I prefer the river to the roads."

Baptiste jumped from his seat. He hadn't realized Father Félicien was still awake. Nodding, his cheeks flushed, Baptiste tried to steady his heartbeat.

"Yes," was all he could think to answer.

"I don't want to sleep," groaned Father Félicien. "I keep having nightmares."

"Oh," said Baptiste, and his concern was genuine.

"Yes," grumbled the Father. "Only the very young and the very old have nightmares. And I'm not in the first group any more."

They chuckled softly amidst the snoring sleepers.

"The roads got worse and worse, didn't they?" recalled Baptiste, trying to converse.

"Oh yes, and worse and worse after that. Thank the Lord for the Ohio River. But things may be getting better up north."

"How do you mean?" asked Baptiste.

"Remember last summer, when we stayed in Fort Duquesne and everything was French?"

Baptiste nodded keenly, "Yes, we came down out of the pass."

"That's it, Fort Duquesne. The people, the food. And

a good church. I would've stayed if she hadn't been so stubborn." He waved at the sleeping Evangéline. "That's where I heard the English were building roads everywhere. Their deputy postmaster is named Franklin. Bob or Ben or something Franklin. He wants roads for the mail."

Baptiste wasn't listening.

"Excuse me, Father. Why do you suppose…? You say she's so stubborn. Well … why is she … so stubborn?"

Father Félicien had been waiting for him to finish his

sentence. Now he smiled and touched his chubby finger to Baptiste's shoulder.

"Are you in love?"

Baptiste was stunned. He couldn't answer, and didn't need to.

"And you have been for many years."

From the prow, Gaston's cry went out again. The Father and Baptiste gazed into a snarled overhang from the riverbank. But no voice replied, only the distant hoot of an owl.

"How could you tell?" whispered Baptiste at length.

Father Félicien smiled mysteriously. "Dear boy, let me tell you...."

"I'm not a boy."

The Father cleared his throat. "Of course not. I forgot. If I belong with the very old, then you must be a grown man."

Baptiste softened.

"She cannot choose," whispered the Father. "Where the heart is strong, the hand must follow, and there's no cure. Let the heart lead and, like a lamp, it will light the way, making things clear that were hidden in darkness."

Baptiste lifted his eyes from the sleeping girl. A solitary moonbeam, like a shaft of silver, quivered through the gloom.

He was nodding. "I know."

Gaston was snoring. Everyone was asleep. Evangéline rubbed her eyes. Her brother had pulled Giselle's cooking bundle down on himself, but it didn't hamper his snoring in the least. She looked around. They were safely moored by the riverbank under a dense canopy of willows, with moss and woodbine trailing into the river. Through the tangled greenery came glints of morning sun, illuminating the water cloaked with a grainy litter from the trees.

There it was again! Yes, a soft lapping sound. She knew this was what had wakened her. From outside, beyond the dark green overhang, came a steady, splashing pulse. Evangéline held her breath to hear better. She didn't dare move. Everyone was asleep, their mouths gaping and their limbs wedged between furs and canvas. She peered through the dangling mosses. They were well camouflaged, for sure. She glimpsed a slow movement in the sunlight, a shadow closing in. *Alligator!* she thought with a sudden chill. *It's seen us!* She wanted to scream out or reach for Normand's gun, but did neither. She just waited, her ears filled with the saucy chattering of squirrels and canaries.

As the shadow glided past their sanctuary, a sigh of relief escaped her. She could see the wheeling stroke of paddles, flicking drops of water at the sun. It was a canoe. A long, broad canoe loaded down with furs and skins. She sat motionless. Who were they? What were they saying? Their voices were low, almost whispering, lost in the shrill patter from the trees. *Pirates.* Gaston had told her about river pirates. She couldn't hear their words, but it wasn't her language or even English. Around her, everyone was asleep. Their best protection was silence. So she sat upright, tracking the gliding shadow with a steady eye. *Holy Father, let the kingdom come in Your name. Give each new day Your blessing…*

The low-slung canoe moved swiftly against the stream. Its prow was turned northward, and sinewy arms made light of the sluggish waters. Half a dozen trappers kneeled with their paddles, peering upstream through dark locks that hadn't seen soap in many a moon. At the helm sat a youth, as dark as the rest. His features had been chiselled by sand and wind, baked by the prairie sun. But deep in his eye, though it stared at the waters ahead, his gaze looked inward, far removed to a silent place. It was no use speaking to him at these times. So the trappers talked with each other.

"*La Rosita dijo que me queria.*"

"*Déjatela! La Dolores es la mejor.*"

The big, square-faced Spaniard called to the youth. "Gabriel, *acércate. Cuál es para té, la Dolores o la Rosa?*"

They didn't really expect an answer. Gabriel was clutching the wide oar, a softness on his rugged brow. In the silence, the others looked at each other, grimacing. Someone choked on a chuckle. The river gurgled to their paddles.

24

"HOLD ON TIGHT!" called Henri at the prow.

They were entering the rapids, the first they had encountered in weeks. Evangéline tried to see over Gaston's shoulder, but to no avail. The river took a good grip on the boat and they surged through the frothy water, shooting past little green islands where cotton trees nodded their shady plumes. A couple of oars were kept in the water to fend off a treacherous rock or sandbar. The river was sputtering and spitting. Evangéline wiped her cheek and squinted to one side, where she could see houses in the shade of China trees, flanked by cabins and dovecots. These were cotton planters of the bayou country. Everyone's spirits soared with the sweeping current. There was a fresh wind in their faces and on both sides the riverbank opened wide on a new view of the Opelousas.

Evangéline clutched the side of the boat. For almost two years her heart had been sustained by a faint vision floating before her eyes. On this same current Gabriel had wandered before her, and each bend of the river was bringing him nearer and nearer.

Behind her, someone was singing.

"Let's go from the beginning
With Robère and his tooth."

Someone else joined in.

"Yes, 'cause it was hurting."

And Henri jumped in.

"It was hurting!"

And Viola was quick to follow.

"It was hurting real bad
When he got on board the ship
At Saint-Malo in old Bretagne."

Their voices rang together on the eddying waters.

"So he bargained with the skipper,
'Monsieur, I beg you, please!'
And the skipper tied a knot
Round poor Robère's tooth
And he brought the string on shore
And tied a sailor's reef
Round the bells of Notre Dame."

Evangéline was laughing. Before she knew it, she had joined in the old ditty.

"So the sails were set to go
And the wind she starts to blow
And the string was tight as fiddle
And the tooth she start to wiggle!"

By now Gaston was standing up, lurching this way and that with the mischievous waters, hurling his mighty bass notes at the clear blue sky!

"And the tooth she start to wiggle!"

Evangéline grabbed him by the seat of his trousers and pulled him down to save him from falling overboard. Amidst bursts of hilarity, the singers went on.

"But it wouldn't let go."

And Thérèse jumped in.

"It wouldn't let go."

And Alphonse, taking her hand in his.

"Nope, it did not want to go!"

Now every last one of them was singing:

"But poor Robère is screaming
And every time he opes his mouth
He pulls the bells of Notre Dame
Till all the church was ringing
And half the town came running
To gawk at all the dinging."

But Henri had dropped out. Evangéline saw him look toward the shore. One by one, they all stopped to listen. Across the water came another voice, deep and full, singing in their own language:

"But the skipper he was stout
And waiting to ship out.
His ship was full of wind and sail
But couldn't get past the pier!"

On the grassy verge of the prairie, they could see a solitary horse and rider. The herdsman was gazing at them from under a broad sombrero, his brown face obscured in shadow. Large and rugged in his gaiters and vest of deerskin, he belted out the words of their own song.

"He walked up to Robère Comeau
And made a ghastly face
And all the screaming turned to laughs

And that was the saving grace!
Robère let up a laugh so loud
He blew his tooth away!
The string let go, the bells were still,
And all the people stared.
Robère Comeau sailed off to sea
Without a one who cared."

Someone whispered, "Basile."

In a flash, the sombrero and the Spanish saddle, the tall stallion and the sun glinting on stirrups were all insubstantial. It was Basile blacksmith of Grand-Pré:

"You see, the saving grace!
Robère let up a laugh so loud
He blew his tooth away!"

With triumphal astonishment, some of them joined in the words:

"The string let go, the bells were still,
Robère was on his way!
He sailed the waves to Acadie
To seek a better day."

The rapids were behind them, and the oarsmen veered sharply to the riverbank, greeting the lone rider with shouts and cheers.

"*Mon Crisse*, it's Basile blacksmith!"

"Basile, *salut bien!*"

"Basile Lajeunesse!"

Evangéline's heart was pounding. As the boat edged sideways to the grassy turf, she was already standing. The keel buffeted against the soft riverbank and in a rush of affectionate clamor, they all stumbled ashore to Basile, who was walking to greet them.

"Henri, *mon Dieu*, you're losing your hair!"

"You would too!" quipped Henri, pointing at Viola who trudged behind with little Hugo.

They had a good laugh, as Viola grabbed his ear in a vindictive squeeze. Gaston came next and then Father Félicien, quite winded, followed by Yvette and all the rest, talking together in a joyous melee of recognition and remembrance.

"You are my guests tonight!" said Basile at last, pointing to a little knoll at the river's bend. "Josie is hanging the wash."

They could see his veranda, overlooking the broad river, the wall shining of whitewash. The rest of the house was shingled with unfinished cypress, the front roof pitched steeply to the peak.

As the crowd shuffled up the slope, Evangéline touched Basile's arm. He turned to see her and his face lit up with admiration.

"Mother Mary, look at you! Every year more beautiful."

Like a part through his left eyebrow and along the bridge of his nose ran the scar where the redcoats had pummelled him. She curtsied, then gave her tongue free rein.

"Dear Monsieur Basile, is he in the house?"

Basile gazed at her, suddenly confused. "*Dieu*, if you came by the swamps, how could you not meet Gabriel?"

Her lip started to tremble, tears pressing at her eyes. "Gone? Is Gabriel…?"

"Be of good cheer, my child. It's only two days ago he departed. Thank God you've come, Evangéline." Basile put his arm fondly around her. "He was not well. Moody and restless, always troubled and sulking, tired of this prairie life when his every dream was of you. He'd go silent for days. He wouldn't open his mouth even to put food in! And then he'd talk of nothing but you and his troubles. No man or woman could stand to be around him, so I sent him to Adayes to trade for mules with the Spaniards."

She had waited so long. She had no more courage to wait. She hid her face on his shoulder and her tears poured onto his vest. He held her in the crook of his arm as they walked slowly after the others.

"Now don't you go wasting your tears or you won't

have any when you need 'em," said Basile warmly. "He's not far on his way. We'll catch him! Up and away tomorrow, my girl, and we'll ride overland and head him off at the Atchafalaya. Bless you, girl, you'll make a person of him again."

25

JOSEPHINE KISSED HER on both cheeks, again and again. Together they prepared the table for supper. It was so good just to listen to the feisty lash of her tongue, invincible as ever. And yet, the two years had made a difference. Evangéline could tell she was walking with some pain, more ungainly, wobbling side to side on stiff ankles. It was the long, damp nights on the ship, no doubt. After all, they had sailed a longer route; right down to the Spanish Coast.

"So that we would never find you again," she said, with flint in her narrow eyes and pride pursing her lips. "That was their plan. Scatter us to the wind, so we'd never find each other and come back for Acadie. But they don't know the half of it! There're many of us left. Just take a good look, girl."

She pointed at the window and there, through the wildflowers, came old Charlot with Michel the fiddler! Behind them followed Denny-on-the-ridge, and Simone with her Maurice, and Giselle walking with Philippe! And many, many more.

"But Monsieur Philippe was in the jail in Halifax!" remembered Evangéline.

"Oh yes. But he was waiting for us on board ship," answered Joséphine, testing the boiling turnips with a knife. "Giselle is very lucky."

Michel Gauthier was tuning his fiddle. There was going to be dancing!

"Be careful with Denny-on-the-ridge," said Joséphine.

"What's wrong?" she asked.

"He wasn't so lucky. His sister took to coughing on the ship and it went to consumption. She never saw land."

His sister from Ile Royale! Poor Marie.

"Just like Monsieur LeBlanc," mused Evangéline.

"René?" gasped Joséphine, staring in disbelief.

Evangéline nodded. They worked side by side, silently tallying the new losses. The other travellers had made themselves comfortable throughout the house and on the breezy veranda. Now they surged forward in a wave of recognition to greet the local arrivals. It was joyous pandemonium!

"Old Charlot wanted to stay with us," said Joséphine. "So now he helps Basile with the cattle. He's well worth his three meals a day. When I saw you coming, I sent him to round up the rest of them. We all live along the river."

Loud cheers and yells came from the veranda as old friends were reunited, splinters of a shipwrecked nation.

"See, there's still life in old tatters!" smiled Joséphine, handing the plates for Evangéline to arrange around the table. "Give me some good ox carts and I'll take us back to Acadie. Now look at that braggart brother of yours! Never told a true tale in his life. We'll need him!" They giggled together. "It'll be Jacques on the blankets with his lame leg. And Michel the pied piper, with half New England skipping along to his fiddle. And Baptiste with his hangdog patience, bless that boy! And Henri with Viola and the kids. All waiting for the old sorrow to let go. And Basile cussin' and roaring when the ox won't pull. We'll be a sight, eh!"

But Evangéline had discovered Yvette sitting alone in

the festive crowd. She was pale and silent. Evangéline set the plates aside and went to her.

"Where is…?" She began, but couldn't go on. "Is Monsieur Normand…?"

Very slowly, Yvette shook her head side to side, giving in to the sobs. Evangéline took her in her arms and felt hot tears wetting her shoulder. She walked Yvette to the veranda where they could sit quietly for a while.

"Was he on the ship with Basile and Joséphine?" she asked.

"No one knows what happened to him," she stammered in a feeble voice.

As Evangéline laid her arms around Yvette, she heard her whisper, "Don't tell Alphonse. Let him be happy tonight."

Everyone gathered around the bountiful table. Joséphine lighted her candles. Basile asked Father Félicien to bless the meal, and then the feasting began. Evangéline strained to join in with the delights of old acquaintance. But her bleeding heart was somewhere else, cowering in a shadow which no amount of candlelight could chase away. She recalled to herself the foreign speech through the tangled vines on the river. *Who had been in that canoe?* The mere thought of Gabriel passing so close, while she alone had been awake to see him, made her sick at heart. Her fear had lost her everything.

"Welcome, my friends," began Basile from the head of the table. "Welcome to a home that's better than the old one! This river doesn't freeze like the Gaspereau. There's no rock to split your ploughshare. It'll run smooth as a keel through water. The orange groves blossom all year long and grass grows more in one night than in a whole Acadian summer."

Murmurs of awe and wonderment were traded around the table.

"Cattle and buffalo run wild. Just take what you need. Farmland and forests forever—yours for the taking. And when your house is built and your field is bursting with harvest, there's no King George to steal your land or burn your barns."

He raised his cup, and the scar across his nose was bright on his dark skin. Everyone tasted the sweet wine. The Acadians were excited. Many of the newcomers were beginning to make plans. Evangéline saw Thérèse and Alphonse leaning their heads together. She smiled. She had lost a sister, but Alphonse would take good care of Thérèse. He wasn't the pest he used to be when they were little.

"I never heard you talk so much," said Joséphine, poking her husband in the ribs. "It doesn't suit you. Why don't you pass that corn to Viola instead?"

There was amusement around the table, as Basile reached for the basket of corn.

"Just making room for your cooking, my *belle*," he said. "The more words I get out, the more beef will go in!"

They all laughed and served themselves of Joséphine's splendid roasts.

"Sometimes I wonder," said Joséphine between bites. "We have all that we need and more, but is it home?"

"What is home?" asked Maurice. "Simone and I left Grand-Pré ten years ago. We thought Beauséjour would be safer. But the French took my farm away because I wouldn't be a soldier. And then Colonel Monckton came and took it all anyway!" The dinner guests were listening. Maurice went on. "I said to Simone, 'Basile's boy is getting married. Let's go home for a visit.' So we did. A week later, we're on the English ships and Grand-Pré is burning! So can you tell me, where is home?"

Many acknowledged the wisdom of his words. Maurice cut another bite from his steak.

"Fire or no fire," said Joséphine, "Acadie is my home." Her voice had a strange tremor.

There were those who nodded agreement. Others listened cautiously. Denny-on-the-ridge wiped his whiskers and leaned into the conversation.

"But Joséphine, just over a hundred years ago there was no Acadie! It was only in the heads of our forefathers, sailing from old France."

"It doesn't matter," said Joséphine. "All of that doesn't matter. It's these hundred years that matter, Denny."

"Everyone speaks French here," began Giselle, a little diffidently. "The Negroes and the French. Everyone. We're safe here. This land belongs to King Louis."

"Maybe," said Simone, "but the English are coming over the mountains." Everyone stared at her. Maurice took her hand. "We heard it down at Boudreau's Landing," she went on. "Just this summer, the English took Fort Duquesne. The French are gone."

"It's now Fort Pitt," added Maurice. "There's no stopping them."

Father Félicien crossed himself, then folded his hands in prayer.

Evangéline, who was sitting beside Yvette at the other end of the table, slipped quietly from her chair and headed for the door. On the veranda, a sweet breath of sage and primrose filled her head and she leaned against a post, letting her eyes wander across the river. The sun had set. The vast reaches of the prairie slumbered near darkness. Where the breeze touched the tall grass, a pale phantom purple would slide across the plain. The horizon had no meaning. The land reached like an opened hand to nowhere. Beside the house, a pair of poplars stood close together. She reached for a leaf and, with a slight tug, severed it from the branch. Rolling it between her fingers, she felt the limp, cool softness on her skin.

Then, in a flash, she knew what God had done. He had plucked her from the tree, just the same way. Just as she was toying with that leaf, He was now toying with her until it was time to let her blow into the desert wind. Rootless. Homeless. Falling. But her cheeks burned with shame for even thinking it! Father Félicien would never forgive her. Her Lord Father in heaven would know her every thought. And so He must. If she was an ungrateful wretch, then so be it. Oh, if only she could have told Papa about the riders in the forbidden forest. But she never did. With her Lord Father, she had to tell all. He must know all that was in her heart.

"Excuse me."

She jumped at the sudden words. But the voice was gentle and familiar. Just behind her, Baptiste was hovering with his hand behind his back. His face wore an appropriate blush. Baptiste *le chien*. *Petit chien*. His droopy cheeks and eyes of melancholy. Deep and gentle eyes, but ever sad. Long before he lost his papa, when they were still children, clutching his hot cider, listening to his papa after school. Even when the stories made him laugh; eyes of melancholy.

"Baptiste," she said, smiling.

"Evangéline," he answered, speaking her full name solemnly.

They stood silent in the dusk, while the lively voices and the lamplight spilled through the doorway.

"I brought you something," he said at length.

She smiled again. "Yes?"

He stretched his hand toward her. She gasped. It was filled with a spray of wildflowers.

"Baptiste.... You picked them?"

"For you."

She took them gently in her hands. "Thank you."

"I could tell you were sad. You and Yvette."

"You're good to me," she said, bringing the flowers to her face to breathe their subtle splendour.

"You lost your papa," he said. "And I lost mine. We could understand each other."

She gazed at him. He was holding his breath, a blushing statue. She turned and looked into the darkness. For two years, she had been sustained by a faint vision floating before her eyes. He was still out there. Somewhere in the night.

"Yes, Baptiste. We understand each other."

She turned to him.

Even his eyes were smiling. "Yes."

He turned and stepped back inside. She was alone with the prairie.

26

EVANGELINE STEPPED into the girdle of Basile's big hands and he hoisted her into the saddle. It was still early and last night's revellers were sound asleep. But Basile was true to his word, and before the sun was up, he had the horses fed and saddled. They were prancing eagerly, steam flaring from their nostrils. Evangéline had not done a lot of riding and never with a Spanish saddle. She clung gingerly to the horse's mane, while Charlot adjusted her stirrups and tightened the cinch. The early sun glittered in steaming grass fragrant with waking flowers.

"God bless!" said Father Félicien, raising his pudgy fingers in a familiar benediction.

"Little sister," called Thérèse from the veranda, "bring him back alive." She looked tousled and sleepy. She had her arms folded around her to keep off the chill.

"*Death to the mercenaries!*" smiled Evangéline, as they waved to each other. Alphonse had to be dead to the world, or he would have been right beside her. Or had he found out about his papa?

Old Charlot climbed into the saddle and took the lead, riding upstream along the misty river. Evangéline touched her heels to the horse and followed, while Basile rode after. Behind their backs, each had blankets, a canteen, and a satchel with bread and Josephine's sausage. Basile's flint-lock rifle hung by the pommel on his saddle. They rode past a small paddock where he showed her the wild horses he was going to break in.

When they reached the open range, Charlot waved his hat and veered off on his own to round up the herds. Out of the grass came the long, white horns of Basile's cattle, like flashes of foam on a tide of green. When they saw the slouched rider approaching, they began to stir, bellowing to each other as they went. It was like watching a sleepy landslide, and Evangéline realized it belonged to Basile blacksmith. He had found a whole new life on the range.

"Do you see the grove of oranges?" called Basile, pointing to a dark, leafy thicket some distance away.

"Yes, I see it," she answered loudly.

"That'll be your house," he said. "And the land down to the river and back as far as you need."

She gazed across the billowing grass.

"Gabriel wasn't at breakfast one day. But he came in from outside and said he'd found just the spot. He'd build you a home over there."

She could picture it. The house where they would have no secrets. A house just for Angels.

"It's a good place," she said.

Basile laughed contentedly and waved her on. There was no time to dally. The shortcut to Atchafalaya River took them across a pathless sea of grass. The wind was their constant companion. They didn't talk much. Basile had his eye on the horizon. Evangéline was tingling with anticipation. The end was only hours away. The end to all her waiting, when her life could pick up and become real again. When she and Gabriel would heal each other's wound and begin a future together. When her hand would clasp his dark curls once more. And they would grow the wings that no one else could see. *Oh Gabriel, you fill my heart, but I cannot see you. You're here, but you're not. How often have you galloped this way to the prairies? When did you lie on this riverbank, dreaming of us? Soon it will be no dream. Soon my arms will have you again!*

The Atchafalaya was a miracle of light that did not fade as they drew near. The river had ballooned into a shallow lake, barely to be seen under a veil of lilies bobbing on the slight noonday undulation. Basile led them part way around the curving shore, where lotuses lifted golden crowns into the sun. The heat was heavy with the scent of blossoming magnolia. On the lake, a little islet glimmered with thick, tangled hedges of primrose, wafting sweet allure across the water. Here was an innocence that preceded man or beast.

"This is not the way we came," said Evangéline in astonishment.

"The swamps are on all sides. And the Teche runs west. You may have passed south of here."

Or else this is all a mirage, she thought. They had arrived at a log cabin next to a simple jetty on rough-hewn poles. Half a dozen canoes lay overturned on the shore. There was no signpost, but Evangéline knew it must be Doherty's Landing. Basile had told her that only Boudreau's was closer to the Acadian farms.

"What brings you up this way, neighbour?" asked the man in the doorway, using his straw hat to wipe sweat from his brow.

"A good day to you, Liam," answered Basile. "I've brought my son's bride-to-be."

Liam Doherty gave a friendly nod of the head.

"We'll just wait for Gabriel to come by."

Doherty now stepped toward them.

"I don't like to argue with you, Basile, but if you're waiting for Gabriel, you'll be waitin' past your bedtime. He was here and gone before breakfast."

Basile stared at Doherty and his brow darkened. "Mother of God, they must be speeding by night!"

He turned to Evangéline with something of embarrassment in his eye. "We should've left the supper last night and rode straight through."

She could think of nothing better than to shrug her shoulders and look down into the saddle.

"Well, we've got the advantage," said Basile. "They have to twist with the river. We'll just cut straight to Adayes."

He handed Doherty some coins for a fresh pouch of tobacco, and they rode on. Evangéline turned to see the water lilies blurring through the grass. It was a mirage. Maybe it hadn't really happened.

She was tired by nightfall. Basile unsaddled the horses.

"Step this way, my girl. Here's something you should learn."

She came and stood by his shoulder, watching him aim a few shakes of powder into the flint-lock chamber of his rifle.

"First bird I shoot tomorrow, I'll get you to load up again. If we're attacked, I'll need both pistol and rifle. You'll have to load as fast as I can fire."

She spread some branches by the campfire and laid their blankets on top of them, to keep the dampness off. *Holy Father, let the kingdom come in Your name. Give each new day Your blessing....* Sleep took her words away.

27

ADAYES HAD ONE STREET. It ran from the river landing and vanished under the grass at the other end of town. The inn was a two-storey edifice of wood and adobe, towering over the adjoining hovels.

"Yes, *Señor*, he was here."

"Are you sure?" growled Basile.

The innkeeper gazed at Evangéline under bushy black eyebrows. "You say you bring the bride?"

Basile nodded impatiently.

"Well," laughed the innkeeper, not unkindly, "then I'm sure! The others went across the street to have some fun. With the girls, you know." He was winking and gesturing. "But he sat right there by the window and wouldn't even talk to me. At least he paid his money, so I wished him good hunting."

Basile made a face of despair.

"So they've turned around already."

"No, no," protested the wide-eyed innkeeper. "He got himself some mules and talked to a couple of Indians. He decided to load up his share of furs and take the road to the prairies."

Basile stood silent. Two flies were chasing each other stupidly in the monotonous heat. Evangéline stepped to the window and sank slowly onto the little bench. Only yesterday, Gabriel had sat in this spot, staring into the mud-baked street. If only she could reach back through one night's darkness, to find his hand on the bench beside her. She would be his pleasure. She would be his

wife. But now she couldn't be sure of anything. Gabriel had struck out on his own, leaving even his papa confused. Who was playing with her so cruelly? Not her heavenly Lord Father? He wouldn't send her such adversity. After coming all the way from Acadie to be with Gabriel, why would He mock her thus? *Oh Gabriel, I'm walking the high rafters alone, and in every swallow's nest I look for the pearly stone that will be our luck. But it's not there, Gabriel. Every nest is empty. When we were little, the pearly stone was always waiting for us. But where has it gone? Who found it? Sweet Lord Father in heaven, keep not my beloved from me. My heart is a desert without him.*

"Which way did he take?" came Basile's question at length.

The innkeeper looked up from his broom. "Seems to me he was taking the Shawnee Trail. North to Red River."

Basile turned to Evangéline. "I don't know these parts. We'll need a scout."

She smiled, and her chest was brimming with thankfulness. "Monsieur Basile ... I cannot say the many thanks I owe you."

"Oh, you don't have to, my girl. I'll catch that scoundrel, don't you fret. Old Charlot will manage my herds till I get back. Or Josie will call on someone to help out." He came over to her. "I haven't forgotten what you did for me once."

"What was that?" said Evangéline.

"When you saved our crop from the mercenaries," he said with a serious demeanor. "When you drowned Acadie. The English didn't get a handful!" He offered her his arm. "And besides, you'll be my daughter by marriage. God strike me dead, if I don't see you settled in wedlock."

They stepped out into the little street to stock up on supplies.

By sundown they were riding far into a new country. The rivers were long gone. Overhead, the sky climbed to a peak of dazzling blue, fretted with fast-blowing cottony clouds. Here was the heart of the prairies, breathing and murmuring in the billowing grass, pulsating between shadow and sunlight. Basile or Evangéline would point to the sky, where a brooding vulture was silently circling to glut on nature's leftovers. Just ahead of them, the olive-skinned Osage guide was tracking Gabriel, forever gliding off and onto his horse like a fish through water. He didn't speak a word of French, but Basile could communicate with him haltingly in Spanish. A couple of hours out of Adayes, Kwapu had spotted a coil of smoke near the horizon. Evangéline couldn't see it, but Basile claimed he did. While they were approaching, the smoke faded to nothing, and now, as the sun was slowly diving into the grass, Kwapu was closing in on his target. He rode ahead, sniffing the wind, gauging its speed, slipping off his horse to read the imprint of hoofs. Evangéline marvelled at the silent skills of this man of the plains. Her back was aching. And her throat was sore from riding into the wind all day.

"Now!" cried Kwapu suddenly.

He was waving his arm and they spurred their horses to a light gallop. When they arrived beside him, they saw the trampled circle in the grass. A pile of charred branches remained from the fire. A pair of whittled wood spits lay close by. One of them held the roasted leftovers of some prairie fowl.

"It's him, all right," said Basile, stepping down to pick up a piece of cloth beside the spits. "That's his bandana."

Before she knew it, she had it clutched to her chest.

Basile smiled at her. "We're on the right track."

He turned to Kwapu and they struggled in their broken Spanish, gesturing vividly. Evangéline brought the bandana briefly to her lips. It had no scent of Gabriel. Instead, it was smeared with cooking grease and had a big hole burned through half of it. That was surely why he had left it. She folded it neatly and tucked it inside her sleeve.

"He says we'd better camp for the night," said Basile at last.

"But...." She caught herself, realizing that Kwapu would know best.

Basile unpacked and unsaddled the horses. Evangéline borrowed his hunting knife and stepped over to the bushes where she could see the marks from Gabriel's blade. Kwapu took his bow and arrows and vanished into the shadows. The sun was down and it was already cooling off. Basile unwrapped his flint and kindling and soon the smoke was rising afresh, the flames crackling on twigs and brushwood.

Evangéline was unpacking the plates when she heard the noise. From somewhere beyond the firelight a shuffling step was approaching. Her heart jumped. Basile stood still as stone. The shuffling came closer. And stopped. In the silence, Evangéline could hear her blood pounding. Where had Kwapu gone? To get out of harm's way? Had he brought them here on purpose?

Had they been riding patiently into ambush and slaughter?

"Kwapu?" called Basile.

There was no answer. Evangéline was shaking like a leaf. She scanned the edge of darkness all around. Maybe they were surrounded. She had heard about this. Would the first arrow find her? Basile had pulled his knife. With his eye on the darkness, he was walking backwards, reaching behind him for the saddle bags. In a flash, he shook the rifle from its sheath and cocked the hammer.

"Watch out, Kwapu, or you're dead," said Basile, aiming his rifle into the night.

Then he looked up from the gun, listening. There was the shuffling again. The plodding steps were coming into the fire's light.

28

SHE WAS SO LITTLE. It could have been a child emerging from the darkness. But her features were lean and chiselled, her brow finely furrowed, her dark lips chapped by the sun. Basile kept his rifle trained on her. Slowly she hobbled toward the fireside, greeting them each with a nod.

"That's far enough," said Basile.

His finger was on the trigger. Evangéline was confused.

"Where are the rest?"

The stranger turned her large black eyes to him, clearly puzzled.

"I'm no fool," he went on. "You're the decoy and your braves are waiting to pounce. But you'll be dead on the ground before they even touch us. You tell them that."

His warlike words echoed in the stillness. She gazed into the surrounding night, then turned slowly to him.

"There's no one out there."

She was speaking their language. Basile stared at her, trading a glance with Evangéline.

"Where did you learn French?" he asked.

"At home," came the gentle reply.

Basile motioned with the barrel of his rifle. "Sit down."

The stranger stepped forward and stumbled. Evangéline reached out to catch her.

"No, be careful," said Basile sharply.

The woman seated herself by the fire. Evangéline stayed on her feet, across from her.

"Are you alone?" said Basile.

"I have told you yes," came the calm, unperturbed reply.

"Where do you come from?" continued Basile, his attention still patrolling the curving edge of darkness.

"I'm going north to my home. I'm a Shawnee," she said, speaking with a quiet, methodical lilt that held them spellbound. "I followed my husband on the river. He was a *coureur de bois* from Canada. We've been to a land of evil, and my husband will never return. The Comanches put him to death. He took many days to die." Her large eyes had no tears, only a glaze of gruesome remembrance. "I wanted only to die. But I escaped instead."

Basile lowered his gun, keeping it close by his feet. He eased himself into the grass near Evangéline. She carved some sausage and reached around the flames.

"Here."

The Shawnee woman ate ravenously. It was impossible to determine her age. She was as lithe as a little girl, yet wearier than old age. Basile was listening for Kwapu's return. When the woman had finished the sausage, she licked her lips and looked up.

"God bless you for this food," she said.

Basile nodded good-naturedly. "If what you've said is true, you're a strong soul indeed. Who is the god that blesses your food?"

She paused for a moment, holding the canteen which Evangéline had offered her.

"I don't know," she said at length. "The dark is full of gods. Manitou is above all. But your God is strong too. The blackrobes have been to our village. They tell us about your God. And other blackrobes are down here also, but I can't speak their words."

Basile jumped for his gun and it went off with a

deafening boom. Evangéline swivelled quickly to look behind her. There, on the edge of the firelight, stood Kwapu with his knees knocking, and a dead rabbit in each hand. It was such a relief that she broke into girlish titters and even the Shawnee woman drew the corners of her mouth into a smile. Basile looked rather awkward as he came around to greet Kwapu. They spoke in Spanish and began to prepare the rabbits for the fire. Evangéline felt the Shawnee woman's gaze. She looked over. It was a gaze such as she had never met before. Nothing menacing or magical, just those large black eyes that had seen everything and seemed to know everything about her. And, surprisingly, it did not bother Evangéline at all.

"Have you heard of Lilinau?" asked the stranger.

Evangéline shook her head.

"Lilinau lived in her father's lodge on the lake of Hurons." Again, her low, melodious voice filled Evangéline with wonder. She didn't even hear Basile's haggling with Kwapu. "Lilinau was fair and wise, and many of the braves would fight a bear just to win her. But she didn't listen to them. She had ears for only one. In the deep hush of twilight, she'd stand by her father's lodge, and in the pines overhead, she'd hear the voice of her lover. Breathing like the evening wind, he'd whisper to her heart such things as made her blush with love and want. That was the courting of Lilinau. But she never saw him, not until the day she was doing her washing in the brook. In a flash, his green plume waved through the forest. She ran to see his face, but the green plume waved and vanished between the trees. She decided to follow him into the forest, deeper and deeper, his breath whispering from every tree. She walked and walked with her heart full of love, nevermore to return. Nor was she seen again by a living soul."

A cold gust crackled through the fire. Evangéline looked up, as from a dream. Kwapu was skinning one of his rabbits.

"We'll have some tender bunny before long," grunted Basile, leaning the loaded spit over the flame. "It's a good thing you found us. Alone in the middle of the night. You must've been frightened half to death."

The Shawnee woman looked at him gently. "The night has no teeth," she said.

Basile pondered her words with a chuckle.

"There's plenty for everyone. I'll bet you could do with a hot meal and a good night's sleep."

She nodded graciously. "I thank you."

The rabbit was browning nicely. Kwapu took out a little reed pipe and began to play softly. But all Evangéline could hear was the wind. The wind always bending the grass, breathing a delicate whisper. The voice of her lover.

29

WEST OF THE OZARK Mountains was a land without grass. Some hardy weeds sprawled across the barren earth; thistle, sage and cactus grew along the trail, but no grass. There were long stretches of sun-baked mud where the parched land gaped deep into the earth. This was the trail that Basile and Evangéline took, following the Shawnee woman. She said most of the northbound traders would stop at the blackrobe's mission before they crossed the desert, and Kwapu seemed to agree. So she rode behind Kwapu, and Evangéline was content to take their advice.

The sun was already far to their left when they rounded a spur of the Ozarks and discovered the tents of the mission. They were nestled among sod-covered pit houses, all part of a native village. These people were of Kwapu's tribe, and he slipped off his horse and was warmly received by his kin. The Shawnee woman pointed toward the back of the village, and Basile nodded to Evangéline. As they rode past the two tents, smoke came from each pit house. Through the smoke hole, a tree trunk notched with steps marked the entrance. Beneath a solitary, towering chestnut tree, they glimpsed the blackrobe with his flock of Osage children. High on the tree trunk behind him, a crucifix was fastened. Christ looked with an agonized face on the lively congregation below. This was their rustic chapel. The young blackrobe was kneeling among the children, speaking animatedly in Spanish to them. He was using little stones on the ground to illustrate some sort of mathematical proposition. Apparently, the lessons went beyond pure and simple catechism. Basile put his pipe in his mouth and sat down to wait for the end of the class.

After a while, the priest folded his hands and turned to the crucifix with a resonant prayer. Basile took off his sombrero. The Osage children looked on with curiosity, joining gleefully in his Amen. The children were dismissed and the blackrobe stood facing them, his hat in his hand.

"God rest you," he said. "I am Padre Alvarez."

Basile used his Spanish as best he could. "My name is Lajeunesse. This is my daughter-to-be. And our friend."

The blackrobe bowed to the women. With a wince, Evangéline noticed that three fingers were missing from his right hand.

"You are welcome. Will you join me for supper?"

They gladly accepted and followed him to a tent where the ground was laid with baskets of corncakes and a crock of brown wine.

"My son Gabriel is riding north from Adayes," said Basile without further ado. "I'm told he had a couple of Osage guides and some packmules loaded with fur."

Padre Alvarez nodded, gazing at them as he munched his corncake.

"Good Padre, this poor girl is betrothed to be his wife, but I can't seem to get the two of them together! Have you seen him pass this way?"

The young priest shook his head, smiling.

"You're on the right track," he answered. "But it won't be easy."

"How so?" rumbled Basile.

"This time yesterday, Gabriel Lajeunesse was sitting on the mat beside me, where your daughter is."

Evangéline clenched her fingers.

"He was telling me this same, sad tale, confessing all his loneliness and useless waiting. Now he said he would run from it all and seek his beloved in the north."

"But he didn't tell me he was going away!" roared Basile, and the young priest cowered on his blanket.

"Only till the end of summer. When the hunt is over, he will return this same way."

Evangéline got to her feet and rushed from the tent. Her head was pounding with sudden, uncontrollable fury. She glimpsed the astonished faces of Osage women and children as she dashed heedlessly to the edge of the prairie. The earth was bone dry beneath her feet. *Who says the Lord isn't cruel!* Who had she been trying to justify? She was searching for her husband and her Lord was turning it into a bad joke, making her misery laughable. What was the use of praying to such a God? Maybe Manitou was kinder. And Glooscap! The great Glooscap had promised to return when his people needed him most. But where was God when Acadians needed Him most? When *she* needed Him most. She dropped her face into her hands, sobbing deeply. *Oh Lord, I can't go on. Are You not my helper? Do You not have an ear for those who pray with their heart? Are You laughing now at my stubborn hope?*

She looked up and gazed into the barren distance, as the breeze plucked a tear from her cheek. Maybe the good god was Glooscap. Maybe Papa had been blind to the truth of Abbé Le Loutre's fight. Maybe it was God's last fight. And they had failed to fight His battle. This, then, was their banishment. The new age of evil. When a true heart would roast on fires of mockery.

"God bless you."

It was Basile's voice, close behind her. Her left foot

was throbbing. She must have stepped on a bone or something in the village.

"Monsieur Basile."

"Yes?" His hand cupped her shoulder.

"You've been so good to me." She rose from her knees and looked him in the eye. "Now you must go home. I'm without a husband, but so is Josephine! And Kwapu's people are kind. With the protection of the missionaries, I'll be safe here waiting for Gabriel."

He met her gaze, thinking it over. She was glad she had spoken so quickly, because already her courage was ebbing.

"Is that your wish, my girl?"

She nodded emphatically, biting her tongue.

"Safe journey, Monsieur Basile."

He came to her with his arms. She surrendered blindly in his huge embrace, as if savoring the last of such girlish comforts. Finally, he held her at arm's length.

"So be it," he said. "The heart in you is too strong. It'll never break. Just keep yourself safe in the mission."

He pulled a leather pouch from his bag, handing it to her. "I haven't counted the coins, but they should see you through the summer. And if Gabriel is late returning, don't give it up. We know what he's like!" He winked at her and she nodded reassuringly.

But he wouldn't go. He brought his big fingers to the tip of her chin.

"Géline," he said. "Always *p'tite* Géline."

Her face smiled, but her heart was screaming. She loved Monsieur Basile, yes, but he was so wrong. Because her heart was not strong! Not anymore! It was already breaking.

30

IN THE MORNING, Basile paid Kwapu for his services and they rode off. They would have each other's company to the south bank of the Arkansas, where Kwapu's village lay to the southwest. But the Shawnee woman stayed. It was a great comfort to Evangéline. For the first time ever, she was on her own. Like one of the cactuses. She gazed toward the windy horizon, where Basile and Kwapu were merging into a wisp of dust. Lone as the cactus.

"Did I tell you about Mowis?"

It was the Shawnee's gentle voice at her shoulder. Evangéline turned back from the prairie, rubbing her face to dispel the stiffness of sorrow.

"No. Who is Mowis?"

The Shawnee woman walked by her side as they returned through the village.

"Mowis was the bravest of the brave. He came to the village in the dead of winter and wooed the Chief's daughter. When he had killed a bear with his hands only, the Chief was ready to give away his daughter. The wedding was at the end of winter, but the next day was spring. When Mowis arose from their bed and stepped out from the wigwam, the sunshine took him by surprise. After just a step or two, he began to melt and dissolve in the heat until his wife couldn't see him at all. She looked everywhere, but Mowis was gone with the snow."

Evangéline walked silently, puzzled and brooding.

"He wouldn't have done well out here," said the woman, nudging Evangéline.

She looked into the Shawnee's black eyes.

"Poor old Mowis would've melted in a minute," she went on, pointing at the searing sun. "Nothing but steam! Can you hear him: 'Whoa, there goes my foot. Where are my legs? Oh no, I'm squishing! Ouch!' "

Evangéline found herself smiling at this graphic picture of brave Mowis.

"Can't you see Mowis dashing to get into the shade! 'Wait—my hands! I'm shrinking. The dogs will step on me!' "

Evangéline gave a soft titter, surprised by her own jolliness.

"He would have a long face when he looked down and saw that the rest of him was gone. A very confused head—and nothing else."

Evangéline was shaking her tresses, helpless with laughter. It was a gift from the woman beside her. How could this voice lead her so assuredly from darkest wonder to brightest whimsy? She wasn't alone after all. But it was not like walking with Thérèse. She was in the company of a friend, a mother and a kindred spirit, all at the same time.

"Do you play checkers?" asked Evangéline.

The Shawnee shook her head. "Checkers, what is that?"

Evangéline walked her back to the smaller tent, where Padre Alvarez had provided them with lodgings. From the bottom of her satchel, she pulled her papa's checkers from Grand-Pré. They found a smooth ledge on the sloping spur of the mountain and settled down. The Shawnee listened keenly as Evangéline explained, recalling for herself the game she had watched by the old hearth.

The fields of maize grew tall with waiting. Summer moved toward harvest. No word came of Gabriel. When it was time to husk the golden maize, the Shawnee woman was still there. Together, she and Evangéline worked with the villagers to harvest the crop.

Padre Alvarez stopped in the field one day, struggling between French and his own tongue.

"Look at this flower." He pointed with his left hand, keeping the other behind his back.

On the ground nearby was a small, unremarkable plant, rearing its head above the cracked earth.

"See how the leaves are turned to the north? It's the compass flower," he said, peering at Evangéline. "God's finger put it here to guide the traveller in the desert. Such, too, is faith. The blossoms of passion shine brightly, but are soon lost. This flower is different. It endures in the wilderness. It's your flower."

She met his gaze. He could be no more than five or six years her senior. What did he know about passion, living his life inside a black robe in the middle of nowhere? But his words were not stupid. Had he known a different life before this?

"Thank you, Father," she said.

Maybe he heard her. He was already walking back toward the village. He didn't turn. Maybe he was too far away.

If Gabriel is late returning, don't give it up. Those had been Basile's parting words. So she waited. Autumn passed and so did winter. Her waiting was made easier by the friendship of the Shawnee. A friendship of few words, often no more than sharing the north wind in their faces, or helping the women prepare pemmican from the catch of buffalo. And a game of checkers on the ledge overlooking the village. The prairie had no snow, only thunder and rain. Whatever the weather, Evangéline would stalk the edge of the prairie, scanning the horizon for a sign. Month by month, her soul was freezing over. She wouldn't quit. Yet something inside her had stopped worrying, as when pain leaves the freezing body long before it is dead. Padre Alvarez would observe her from his tent, with pity swelling in his chest. The Shawnee would take her arm and turn her away from the stark landscape, to simpler distractions.

Well into the spring, another blackrobe, somewhat older, arrived from the north with native guides. As Padre Alvarez sat down to dine with his new colleague, he asked directly about Gabriel Lajeunesse. The Father shook his head but called for his guides. It was a good thing. They were of the Winnebago people living by the St. Lawrence. One of them remembered a young Lajeunesse.

"Where did you see him?" asked Evangéline.

The Winnebago had enough French words to answer her.

"South. We go from Adayes to hunt the beaver. To hunt the moose."

Evangéline stared. This was one of the guides she had trailed with Basile and Kwapu a year ago.

"Do you know where he is?" she stammered.

The Winnebago gave a nod.

"Hunting very good. Young Lajeunesse is happy at Saginaw River."

Padre Alvarez reached over and touched her shoulder.

"God has blessed you. This man is the Lord's messenger. Go with him when he returns to his people."

31

ONLY DAYS LATER, Evangéline broke up her lodgings at the mission, saying many farewells to the young blackrobe and the Osage villagers. She followed the Winnebago guides toward the distant St. Lawrence. Much to her comfort, she had the company of the Shawnee, who chose this opportunity of escort to return to her own people. It was a journey of many weeks. As they rode farther, familiar trees greeted them, closing endlessly into a forest of spruce and hemlock, of tamarack and pine, such as Evangéline had nurtured in her memories of home.

Without warning, the Shawnee woman turned to her and pointed to the east. "I must go home."

They were in the middle of nowhere, but she knew where she was. As on that first night when she had stumbled up to their campfire. She was at ease in the dark. The night had no teeth. She had been half destroyed by the enemy, but she was not lost. Her quiet, melodious voice knew the way. How would Evangéline live without it?

"I wish you a happy return," was all she could say.

But the Shawnee woman reached over and handed her a leather sheath with a hunting knife.

"Ride with Manitou. I'll be in my wigwam soon."

Evangéline clutched the weight of it in her hand. Her chest was heaving. "We've been together so many moons. But I don't know your name."

The Shawnee smiled mischievously. "Lilinau."

Their eyes met. Evangéline smiled back. The moment was past, and now the Shawnee was riding into the forest, a breeze lifting her shining hair.

"*Adieu!*" called Evangéline, waving.

The Shawnee looked around and waved. Then she was gone into the bushy gloom. Nevermore to return. It was so simple. And so very difficult. One of the horses whinnied, pricking up its ears. The Winnebago guides sat immobile, waiting. It was time. Evangéline set her thoughts on Gabriel and they rode on, following the Illinois River to the shores of the great lake.

Evangéline gave to the guides all that was left in her purse. They saluted her and rode west toward their own lands. On a sheet of bark, they had carved the curving of the lakeshore. Evangéline was to follow it to the Potawatomi trail, then cut across to the Saginaw River. Half a day's journey downstream, she would see Gabriel's lodge. The long blade was at her side. At night, she crawled into the deepest shelter of a fallen tree and slumbered uneasily, her hand on the knife.

The darkness was pressing on her eyes. To one side she caught a movement, soft as a shudder. With a wince, her eye followed and fixed on a shadow that was no shadow.

"Monsieur Basile!" she cried out.

The old blacksmith was lifting his feet through the underbrush, steadying himself against a maple. She stepped toward him.

"How did you find me?"

"Silly questions, my *p'tite* Géline," he smiled.

She noticed that he wasn't alone. Just behind came old Charlot, hands in his pockets, toothless cheeks flapping at each breath. And coming in the other direction she could see her brother Gaston, with a knapsack over his shoulder.

"How many shovels do you need to bury an Acadian?" he mumbled. But he wasn't smiling. He was contemplating his own question. "How many shovels…?"

A lone candle flickered in the dark woods. Approaching her in his black robe, Abbé Le Loutre held the flame in front of his face. "And die she did," he was saying, "hanged according to law. But in the scales of justice, a magpie had her nest. And woven in its walls was the necklace of pearls. Behold the stolen pearls!"

He halted in front of her. His features were glistening with sweat, his eyes like embers glowing in the ashes of his face. Behind him, she glimpsed Basile and Charlot and others kneeling. She followed their example. The Abbé held the candle aloft in a secret benediction. Once again, her nostrils were filled with his strong breath. Around his waist, she discovered a belt hung with scalps. One of them was more than a scalp. It was the entire head, lopped off at the neck. It was Gabriel, hanging from Le Loutre's belt, looking at her with dim surprise. Blood was still trickling from the neck. *Le Loutre's blood*. From Gabriel's neck, but it was Le Loutre's blood. The dark drip plopping into her lap. It was strong blood, strong enough to swallow her. Everywhere the drip landed, her skin began to melt, dissolving into air, fading into night. Her knees and arms were melting, she was no longer there. Only her eyes were left and they had no feeling. Gabriel's mouth was moving as if to speak, but only a scream could get past his lips and it was her own voice screaming.

She rubbed her eyes. The trees were silent, waiting for her heartbeat to settle. In her nose, the sharp odor of skunk. The little animal was digging and poking for something among the leaves nearby. Her hand was still on the knife. She dared not go back to sleep.

The leaves had turned russet and gold by the time she arrived at the little waterfall on the river. A drizzling rain pattered in the trees. The mosses were deep and dank. It was no great shock to her, seeing the cabin in ruins. The inside was ravaged and deserted. She poked around in the remains, hoping for some token of Gabriel. Nothing was left. Only the musty smell of abandonment, and squirrels scuttling between broken floorboards. The rain splattered in her face through a break in the roof.

"Gabriel!"

She called his name once.

No one knows where Evangéline went. Her heart stepped over the edge into a great void. And her feet followed. She had no direction left. She had no knowledge of the woods, except what Papa and Gaston had shown her. She had spent the last coin from Basile's pouch. Her horse plodded steadily toward the east. She knew no names, no roads; only the sun. Early in the day, she would steer for the light; later she kept it behind her. It was the picture of her life, repeating itself each day. At secluded trading posts or in noisy camps of the army, she lingered briefly to watch and wait. Those who saw her could only pity her. There was no life left in those eyes. Gone was the spark that made mowers and reapers sing in old Acadie. The lone waif on the big Mexican

steed was an enigma to those who saw her pass. A
mystery that was better left alone.

"Lookin' for something?"

When she turned, the young officer stepped closer.

"Can I help you, ma'am?" he asked. The young man
touched his glove to the brim of his hat in a smart salute.
His sparkling eyes of blue over a well-waxed mustache
made her gasp.

"Don't mean to startle you, ma'am, but I saw you
watching the soldiers for an hour or more."

Behind her, the captain called "Charge!" once more,
as the new recruits pressed their horses to a gallop,
drawing their sabres to maim the dirt bags up ahead.

"Waiting for your husband?" asked the officer, still
smiling.

She looked up at him, wincing. "Why do you say
that?" she stammered.

He put up his hands apologetically. "Begging your
pardon, I don't mean to be nosey but I couldn't figure
what else you'd be doing out here all by your little
lonesome."

She held his gaze briefly, then looked down.

"One of Captain Rawlins' men, is he?"

She shook her head.

"Why, then you've got the wrong camp," said the
officer. "I'm Corporal White. Stanley White. If I can be of
assistance…."

"Maybe my husband isn't a soldier."

The young corporal remained silent, pondering her
words. At length, he stepped a little closer.

"If you don't mind, ma'am, what would be his name?"

"Lajeunesse," she answered softly. "His name is
Gabriel Lajeunesse."

The corporal's eyes began to shine, as he shook his head side to side. "Now if this ain't the darndest bit of providence! You know who is visiting from Fort Wayne?"

She looked at him again. "Who?"

"You guess."

"Who?" she said again, drawing a deep breath.

"You tell *me!*" he answered, and now he was getting excited, slapping the hat on his knee. "C'mon, who do you think?"

She stared at him, unable to speak. A winning smile behind the broad mustache, he offered her his arm.

"To Corporal Lajeunesse, step right this way!"

She wanted to go with him but her knees were folding. *Corporal.* Gabriel a corporal!

"I know, I know! It's too good to be true. You can come or you can stay, but he's having a snooze right over there in the last tent."

Corporal White was pointing her to the end of the muddy aisle between the dingy canvas tents. Evangéline reached back and stroked her big Mexican over the muzzle. He reared his head gently into her hand. Then she slipped her fingers around the corporal's proffered arm and trudged with him to the tent.

She couldn't see anything at first.

"Take a look at this," said Corporal White, dropping the tent flap behind them.

She thought he was speaking to her. But her eyes opened to the dark, and saw that he was talking to a dim figure rising from his stool to face them. He was a large man in a drab greatcoat which cloaked his body like a hairless carcass. As he stepped toward them, she saw a mouth full of teeth the size of bullets. She squinted into the shadows.

"Where is he?"

The corporal was right behind her. "You're looking at him."

She gasped, as the stranger loomed over her. "No, it's.... It's not...."

"Don't worry," smiled Corporal White at her ear. "He'll be whoever you want him to be." So saying, he took a firm hold of her wrist.

"But, sir, you don't understand...."

The stranger put a huge hand to her chin, pressing his thumb over her lips. It reeked of stale tobacco. "Hush, little lady. This is no way to treat friendly folk like me and the corporal. Isn't that right, Stanley?"

She glanced over and saw the young corporal's eyes, still sparkling.

"Please, where is my husband?"

"Hear that?" whispered White. "Doesn't she sound kind of French or something? Thought you might be interested."

The hulking hands of the stranger inspected her face, her teeth, her hair, groping carelessly.

"I need strong girls," he mumbled, purring deep in his throat. "Once they get too run down, the price drops."

"But they'll pay good for a French accent," urged the corporal.

Evangéline felt her legs giving way. Her stomach was ready to come up through her mouth. She lurched sideways, jabbing her shoulder into the corporal's chest, but he was ready for her. He twisted her arm to her shoulder blade and held her captive.

"Even so!" purred the cloaked stranger appreciatively. "She's still got some go in her. I think you've got yourself a deal."

32

HER BODY WAS ICE. How could she save herself when her arms and tongue wouldn't move, when her legs wouldn't carry? Corporal White's blue eyes were eating her alive. His arm was strapped around her so that she couldn't get her breath.

"Isn't it a joke!" he was saying. "You come all the way from St. Louis to give us your girls. And here in the bush, I find you such a little dandy, all lost and forsaken."

The stranger was counting up some coins. "Three pounds, and don't complain!"

The corporal pocketed his coins.

"You'd best be out of here. Captain Rawlins will be back from the ridge."

The other man showed his teeth in a yellowed grin, stepping to the entrance. "Let me collect for the other girls. I'll be right back." He noticed that Evangéline was shaking as with a fever. "I'll find you a good classy establishment. Get you all washed and scrubbed. Call you Lolo or somethin'."

The tent rocked as he scrunched himself through the opening and was gone. The corporal had her hand pinned between her shoulder blades. He walked her toward a cot in the corner.

"Next time I'll know to send for Lolo, eh. Lonesome little Lolo!"

It was a bad dream, scraping bluntly through the door of her wildest imagining. And it wasn't ending, like the other ones. She couldn't wake up. He gave her a shove and she collapsed on the blankets.

"Just a little fun before you leave me," smiled the corporal, unbuckling his holster.

The impact from her fall had roused her. She opened her mouth wide but before the scream got out, his hand clamped down on her face. His mouth was right beside her now.

"I'll kill you if you do. See, the Captain won't have any of this." He was picking at her clothes. "He'd have me over a barrel and fifty lashes laid on. A comrade of mine even lost his stripes, imagine that!"

His hand was everywhere, touching her where Gabriel had never touched, or even Maman or Papa or anyone. In a haze, her rage came rushing from deep down. It was the Shawnee riding out of the forest, a breeze lifting her shining hair. Ride with Manitou. *Ride with Manitou!* Suddenly she clutched the weight of the hunting knife.

"Ride with Manitou!" she sobbed mutely into the tight seal of his hand, her arm swinging wide and driving the blade hard into Corporal White's back. With a groan he rolled sideways, his weight just missing her. Not knowing what to do with the dripping knife, she held it tight as she scrambled to her feet. Behind her, White was trying to say something. Crashing against a rack of uniform jackets, she staggered to the entrance. She ran for her life, lurching and slipping through the mud. Everything all around was a blur. There were footsteps and men's voices, but no sound of alarm. A wide-eyed soldier stepped out of her way as she reached the horse. She clasped the pommel in her hands and pulled herself up into the saddle. The Mexican steed whinnied contentedly. Evangéline threw a glance backwards along the aisle. At the last tent, she saw the great hairless carcass stooping to step inside. She made sure the knife was firmly in her boot. Then she dug her heels into the horse's side and headed for the trees. The wind lifted her shining hair.

It must have been May or June when she rode into the mountains. There was still snow on the high slopes, but the valley was bursting with leaves. She had seen these mountains before. A long time ago, the Acadians had loaded their caravan of ox carts at Baltimore, and taken to the trail. Up the Potomac Valley to the steep slopes. She had never known a mountain before. That same rugged calm came back to her. "General Braddock's road," she recalled Alphonse explaining.

"Who is he?" she had asked.

Alphonse had rolled his eyes. "Do I know everything? It's his road, that's all."

She stroked her horse's silvery neck. Where was Alphonse now? And Thérèse? And everyone. Her path skirted a wide plateau rising steeply above the valley. She reined in her horse and gazed over the edge. The clouds rolled away and she could see rivers like ribbons of blue stretching many miles toward the sun. In the heart of the valley was a large town where the rivers came together. She had been there. She knew those rivers. She had been so keen to learn a name for everything. The Ohio. The Allegheny. And the third was too long to remember. But she knew the town. It was Fort Duquesne, where Father Félicien had been so content.

From the sky, a mournful, honking salute descended upon her head. She turned and squinted at the sun. It was the geese. Streamers of wild geese, with summer

trailing from their taut necks, winging their way to distant shores in Canada. As she gazed on the town, her mind's eye plucked all the French away from the streets and put English instead. *Fort Pitt*. That was the news, wasn't it? It had become Fort Pitt. Whatever God had done, He hadn't done it just to her. They were all slaves to His plan.

Very thinly through the liquid air, she heard the rushing of the rivers. Undying joy of the elements, flowing toward summer once again. A soft breeze touched her cheek with fragrance of spruce and balsam. She unlaced her jacket. As she looked down the broad valley, her head cleared like the sky and in that radiant solitude she saw the world not so dark, but shining with love. The whole world, not just Gabriel. She saw the long road she had come, smooth and shining now. *Adieu, Gabriel*. The rivers whispered to her. Somewhere out there, Alphonse and Thérèse were whispering. And Gabriel. And Papa and Maman, together. Gaston too. Even Lilinau had returned to her, riding out from the forest with a wind in her hair just when Evangéline thought she was lost to shame. They would whisper from their many valleys. There would be a whispering of people in her blood. Everywhere, in all things, Gabriel was alive. And everything she could ever give to someone, would be a gift to Gabriel. A gift from the love that had been theirs.

For so many moons, she had been blaming her Lord for their misfortune, as if all humankind were mere infants or earthworms wriggling on the floor of His Creation. But as she gazed upon Fort Pitt, she knew that the real perpetrators of history were men, not gods. God was not a captain. His power was to inspire, not to command! Only by shutting their eyes to Him, could men put a torch to Grand-Pré, or snatch a young man from his bride, or scatter a people into the wind. These were the mercenaries. They had the genteel face of Colonel Winslow, rotting from inside. *Death to mercenaries!* God's power was not to rule the world, but to inspire the world. "When we're too old to live, that's God who stops giving." Papa had said that. "But to take life from the young is to work for the Devil." Those were his words, when Abbé Le Loutre had held a gun to her head. "So we must refuse to fight. We must stick to the chores that God has for us."

The chores of God, she thought. And while she watched the geese melting into the blue yonder, a new thought came to her. *Lord Father in heaven, let the kingdom come. Forgive my rash blames, and let me not accuse wrongly again.* She remembered their first winter away from home, in the poorhouse of Philadelphia. *Let me follow the steps of Your Son, our Saviour. In the city of brotherly love, Your disciple William Penn built a Society for Friends. Let me serve You as they do. Let Your inspiration fill the streets and change the lives of all men.*

33

SHE HAD A WINDOW. Beneath her low ceiling, a small window peered up to the cobblestones of the adjoining street. All the rest was underground, which was a blessing in winter. She was thankful for her own place, not having to share with other boarders like most of the Friends she had met. She could walk a few steps along each wall. That was the extent of her space, underneath a butcher's shop. And she blessed Mr. Hillyer every morning for taking her in. In return, she scrubbed the bloodied blocks after his day's work.

At Christmas, Evangéline begged the bones and innards from Mr. Hillyer's chopping block and cooked a broth to serve to the homeless. Mary and Bryan came from Mr. Penn's Society to lend a helping hand. It was a feast without compare. For weeks to come, starving souls all through Philadelphia would shut their eyes against the bitter wind and remember Christmas, embellishing the story as it passed from mouth to hungry mouth. It was the night in Appletree Alley. It was the night Karl showed up with his accordion. Yes, and Jasper had his spoons out and everyone took to dancing in the falling snow.

"But Philadelphia isn't yet a hundred years old," said Bryan as he dipped his ladle in the steaming broth to serve the next person.

Old Paddy had his helping, cupped in his hand for warmth. In the other hand was his bottle of gin.

"I was in these streets when you were in the willy-wally cradle!" said he, flourishing the soup and the gin, and undecided between them. "And trust me, laddie, there's more than a hundred years on this street. Aye, nothing gets as old and stale as a street."

Evangéline overheard them. She was slicing the crumbly corncake for the soup line.

"But we were the founders of this town," said Mary proudly. "We know our history."

"Ach, do you now?" smiled Paddy. "Maybe I don't mean history so much. Maybe I mean crowding of the soul." He peered at her with a mischievous challenge in his eye. "I once lived in a valley. Each rainfall would scrub the world clean, start you over from Adam and Eve. Streets never get clean like that. They just pile up with bad memories."

Karl had finished his broth and went back to the accordion. Many a soul stepped into the street to shake a leg. The gentle snow egged them on.

But Evangéline was thinking. Back home, it was true, the grass had been a healer. Her pain or her anger, swearwords or cheating, even the shame of thinking how Father Félicien could resemble a bullfrog—all would subside into the grass, receding into nature. Rain would wash it clean. Her heaviest tears had turned to flowers in the spring. But here the grass was buried under the city. Cobblestones and boardwalks had shut the door on nature. Filth and tears and bloody violence were trapped forever on the surface, staining the curbstones and sewers, the walls of brick, the very air she breathed. Nothing could disappear.

While thinking thus, her ears were touched by a golden voice.

"And I wished I was in sweet Dungloe
And seated on the grass
And by my side a bottle of wine
And on my knee a lass.
I'd call for liquor of the best
And I'd pay before I would go
And I'd roll my Mary in my arms
In the town of sweet Dungloe."

Old Paddy had put away his bottle and was teetering on top of a crate, arms spread like angel's wings and his mouth opened wide. Lord, what a voice in that man! And there was broth and corncakes galore. Christmas had come!

Mr. Hillyer was so pleased to find himself the benefactor of so many, that he invited Evangéline upstairs to dine with his family. So she laundered her clothes and washed her hair and donned her white Norman cap. Then she walked up through the shop, took the stairs to the top of the house, and knocked. She curtsied to his large wife and his five daughters, almost her own age. Mrs. Hillyer showed them in turn.

"This is Amanda. And Lottie. And this is our little Holly. And this is Chloris. And this is Beatrice."

Evangéline was bobbing up and down, as she curtsied to each. Mrs. Hillyer guided her through a small, well-appointed parlor into the dining room. Tapers gleamed everywhere, filling her head with the warm glow of Holy Sabbath. The daughters were gleefully forming a ring around the riches of the table while Mr. Hillyer seated himself at the end. They bowed their heads while he said grace, and then the girls grabbed eagerly for the turkey and the potatoes, the squash and the cranberries.

"Patience, patience!" called Mrs. Hillyer. "Little Evangéline is our guest, don't forget."

Lottie made an awkward face and handed the dish of vegetables to the guest.

"Are you happy here?" asked Mr. Hillyer, tucking the napkin under his chin.

"Yes, sir," she said, nodding as she spooned the steaming carrots onto her plate.

"You don't say much, that's why I ask," he replied jovially.

"I'm happy. I don't know many words to speak."

"Nonsense, you dear child," broke in Mrs. Hillyer, "you sound more like an Englishwoman every day. You don't have a thing to worry about." She took a piece of white meat on her fork, turning it in gravy. "Mr. Hillyer is very fond of you. And you're such a worker, Evangéline."

"Thank you, Mrs. Hillyer," she answered, uncertain if it would be proper to take another bite.

"I guess your women are different from your men," chuckled Mr. Hillyer.

She looked up with a smile.

"Excuse me?"

"I mean that your women are used to hard work."

Now Evangéline had to swallow hard. Something troublesome was stirring deep inside of her.

"And our men too," she said.

"Well ... of course," rallied Mrs. Hillyer sweetly, passing her the dish with stuffing. "Aren't you sweet!"

"Thank you," said Evangéline, clutching the dish hard. Then she heard herself ask, "Why are our men not good?"

All the daughters had stopped eating, fork or knife at the ready, as they peered in her direction. Mr. Hillyer was pursing his lips for a sip of port.

"Gracious me," he grunted, "did I embarrass you? It's nothing! We're getting to know our immigrants, is all. And everybody knows the French Neutrals are hardworking women."

"And the men too," repeated Evangéline quickly, her eyes downcast. "My papa had a...."

"Yes, yes, dear child," intervened Mrs. Hillyer, beaming energetically. "Such a clever girl. Now don't you let that turkey get cold. Chloris, have some carrots! Garnet, dear, would you pass the butter."

The butcher handed her the butter urn.

"What was Buddy Stevens saying the other night?" he persisted. "And Mayor Price after church?"

"What about, dear?" asked Mrs. Hillyer, not very convincingly.

"About the French Neutrals. You know, the menfolk."

"Oh that!" Mrs. Hillyer was munching vigorously, to see if that might halt the conversation.

But Evangéline was overcome with old and distant feelings. Nothing could stop her now. Mr. Hillyer laid his fork down with a clink.

"Is it true, young lady, that they don't clear any trees? They just let the woods grow and fence off the ocean to get their land for free?"

Evangéline was clutching her fork and knife. "Excuse me, sir.... Maybe you don't know that...."

"I should certainly think," chirped Mrs. Hillyer, "that little Evangéline was too young to remember much about her homeland, isn't that so, dear?" She gazed at Evangéline with a plea to drop her husband's challenge.

"It's not easy to build a dyke," she said softly, almost inside of herself.

The Hillyers gazed at her, all their eyes intent in the candlelight. The ample Mrs. Hillyer broke into a soft laugh.

"There now, listen to that! Hardly a trace of Acadian."

"It's not easy to build a dyke!" snapped Evangéline again, and her words stuck like daggers in every wall of the room. Her knuckles were white.

There was an astonished silence. At length, the butcher wiped his sodden lips with the napkin.

"Take our plates to the kitchen, girls. It's time for pudding."

The daughters pushed back their chairs and scurried.

"Oh ... is it?" Mrs. Hillyer looked confused. "Why yes, of course!"

She waved to Amanda to fetch the pudding from the pantry. Leaning toward the butcher, she half-whispered, "And don't you worry, Garnet. Little Evangéline means well. All she needs is encouragement."

Evangéline stared at the table cloth, drained and tired unto death. In the warm glow of many tapers, she tasted her first plum pudding.

Through winter's dreary cloak, the new year called out to Evangéline. In the evenings and late into the night, she would roam the streets, with or without the company of Friends, to visit the hideaways of the homeless or the old and the sick in their drafty garrets. At their bedsides she would sit alone, or with a fellow Friend, listening as they unburdened their hearts or squeezing their hands in comforting silence. Whenever she could coax a smile or a hopeful thought from their

lips, her own spirit would quicken. She would light her
candle and set it nearby. *Gabriel? In the eye of the flame,
smiling over your shoulder? Smiling to me as you dropped my
hand and walked to the ships. Now and ever. Amen. The years
have no power to change you. Burning so slowly, deep in my
heart. I grow wings. Be Angels with me.*

Night after night, when the world was asleep, as the
weary watchman called through the streets that all was
well, high at some lonely window he would see the light
from her candle. Day after day, in the grey dawn, as Mr.
Hillyer was unbolting his shop he saw that pale, sweet
face returning from long vigils. When she was dead
tired, the town was like a phantom around her. Her eyes
weren't used to these looming walls of brick, often three
or even four storeys high. Nothing was left of the horizon;
she was surrounded. She gazed with wonder as she
passed Christ's Church at Mulberry. She had never seen
anything so noble and buttressed. It was the living
picture of all Father Félicien's words about the old
cathedrals of Notre Dame. And she would breathe
deeply of all the smells from shops, warehouses, and
offices along Market Street, with the private homes up
above. She used to take the turn past Mr. Penn's great
Meeting House. She looked inside once, when Mary and
Bryan asked her to join the Society. It was very big
inside. Maybe she would join, but it was very big.

At the end of a long night, the candle could smooth all
sorrows from her brow. Through the winter, that timid
flame became her closest friend. *Burning so slowly, deep
in my heart. Is it you?* Her window didn't do much to
brighten the room. The crisp thunder of wagonwheels
rattled the glass. Busy boots or clogs clicked along the
cobblestones. Barking dogs, urinating at her wall. Cats

howling with cold. Drunkards roaring their rage when no one would open a door to them. Muffled shocks of a boot kicking a baffled body again and again, in broad daylight. This was the life Evangéline heard. She pressed her eyes shut. If that wasn't enough, she covered her ears. *Gabriel? Be Angels with me.*

But on the first of May, Mr. Hillyer loaded Mrs. Hillyer's three bulging picnic baskets on the wagon. He invited Evangéline along and she stepped in the back, with all the gushing daughters, and they drove up the sunny side of Chestnut Street. She marvelled at how different the world looked from her perch on the wagon. She hardly noticed the sights and sounds that had crowded in through her little window. They drove all the way to Glouster Point and had a whimsical afternoon in the woods. It was near dusk when Evangéline took Mr. and Mrs. Hillyer by the hand and curtsied deeply, to thank them for such a rare day. The daughters were a little embarrassed. They rushed blithely upstairs, while Evangéline lingered briefly above ground.

34

WALKING OFF THE BIG SHIPS were travellers from near and far, speaking Irish and German, Dutch and Scottish and Swedish. But only rarely French. Whatever they spoke, they were asking about the mountains and the Ohio River. Except for those who were too weary or too sick, those who were consumptive from the crossing or delirious with smallpox and dysentery. And then there were the dreamers who would never be ready for the new land. All of these had to settle for the gutters of Philadelphia. They became the vagrants, the disenfranchised, the rabble who dined with the rats. They never lived long. In the streets of Philadelphia, death grew triumphant. A plague was overtaking the living, heaping corpse upon corpse; wealth had not the power to bribe, nor beauty to charm. The yellow fever was claiming everyone alike. And those who were poor or homeless, with no one to care for them, found their last comfort in the old Alms House.

On the edge of town, the Alms House lay nestled between meadows and woodlands, safely removed from the frowns of well-to-do townsfolk. Many of Mr. Penn's disciples frequented the Alms House to spread good cheer and pray for the sick and the dying. Early or late, they were likely to find Evangéline there, helping the fevered inmates in their final hours.

She never missed a Sunday. After prayer, she would fold her boiled towel into the pocket of her skirt, step into her clogs and blow out the candle. It was late August now and summer had passed like a cruel tease through the streets of death. She crossed the canal where chattering boys were hunched over their bobbing fishlines. As she turned her steps up the cobbled Market Street, her brother came into her mind. Gaston the fisher. Where had he settled? Who was left from the days of old? She rarely dreamed of Acadie anymore. Even Papas's face had drifted from her view. She yearned to see the creases of his smile, but it wouldn't come. The effort of her new life had power over the old days.

She found High Street and walked past the stately Meeting House. Breathing deeply of the maples, she brushed a tear from her cheek. She had seen too much since the sailing of the ships from Grand-Pré. All along the way she had buried something of herself. Was there anything left? What was the use of remembering?

At Appletree Alley, she passed the barn-like majesty of the Lutheran church, and across the meadows came the singing of the Swedes from their church at Wicaco. Between the warehouses, she had a glimpse across the Delaware, with the golden sandspit of Pettys Island.

Down the little slope she walked, to the grove of maples. She stopped to pick some wildflowers between the trees. Their fragrance would give some joy to those inside. The corridor of the Alms House was dark. From her pocket, she brought the towel to her face and tied it over her nose and mouth. Through the doorway on the left, she stepped into the ailing crowd. An odour of sweat and naphtha penetrated through her towel.

From all around came the forced breathing and groans of ebbing life. On crude pallets or on the floor, bodies huddled in contortions of fever and pain. She quickly made her rounds, noting to herself how swiftly inmates had vanished to the graveyard, and in their place new faces, always with death in their eyes. She passed gently between the pallets, moistening a feverish lip or an aching brow, closing the sightless eyes of the dead. She gazed in wonder at the covered bodies, like drifts of snow by the roadside. Through the window came the chimes of distant bells from Christ's Church. Death had laid his hand upon so many a heart and healed it forever.

Something twitched within her and she had to look again. What was there in that twisted neck and that unshaven jaw that drew her closer? Some subtle distinction memorized forever in the heart. A sculpting of the cheek and a curve of the brow that seized her, nudging her to come close. She stood for a long while like one who has lost her senses. The wildflowers slipped from her grasp. Her lips went dry against the towel. Her head was reeling with certainty. She had not the power to move, yet her heart was pounding madly. She gazed upon a withered face, ghostly and sunken with fever, framed in long abandoned locks of hair. He was breathing, but sinking already toward the darkness. Her heart put a name to the image and slowly her lips moved.

"Gabriel."

35

IT WAS HIS FACE. Scarcely two feet from hers. It was his arm, listless against the floor. And his breath, struggling in stuttered, wheezing moans. Quickly, she removed the towel from her face.

"Gabriel," she whispered again.

But her words came nowhere near his pain. He was sinking deeper toward darkness. His forehead glimmered with beads of sweat. She reached for a rag and dabbed his brow. Hesitating for a moment, she brought her hand to his face and laid it gently over the eyes. There was a flutter in his eyelids, but he was too far away. She left her hand there and shut her own eyes. Time reeled her away toward a distant shore in the depths of her heart. It was her own Gabriel!

His face was burning, so she soaked a fresh rag in a pail of water, folded it, and draped it over his forehead. She brought out her candle and lighted it. Then she pulled up a little stool by the bedside. Her forehead rested on her folded hands. *Holy Father, let the kingdom come in Your name. Now at last I find him, so take not Gabriel away from me. Let me live as his wife. Amen.* She opened her eyes and gazed at his ashen face, and she knew it was asking too much of her Lord. If He was going to send miracles, He would have sent them a long time ago.

At dusk, she still hadn't moved. His hand was between her hands, limp and heavy. It had been a clear day and the light was sinking into the Skuylkill River beyond the meadows. The evening sun touched his face with a warm glow as if to mock his former vigour. Bright on his lips burned the flush of fever as if life, like the Hebrew, had smeared his portal with blood, so that the Angel of Death might see the sign and pass over. She had been replacing his wet cloths with fresh ones, then briefly ministering to the others who had need, returning eagerly to Gabriel's bedside.

As she sat studying the mute features of his face, her heart began to see again. She saw the green meadows of long ago, the landscape of her oldest dreams. Village. Hillside. Woodlands. The dykes and the forbidden forest. And standing in the falling snow, her first kiss from Gabriel. Her fingers in the curls at his ear. Between her palms, his fingers were moving. She looked up.

"It's me," she said, breathless.

His eyes opened and met her gaze. She would have smiled if she could. He stared at her flatly.

"I'm burning," he said slowly.

She nodded, unable to speak.

"Where are we going?" he whispered.

"Nowhere. God brought you to me. He will not take you so soon."

Her voice seemed to clear Gabriel's head.

"You're not a ghost."

She squeezed his hand, shaking her head.

"Mother of God," he whispered through parched lips. "It's you."

She leaned forward to remove his rag and laid a fresh one in its place. He just lay there, wheezing with disbelief.

"I have no time," he said at last.

"We are Angels," she answered him quickly.

The fever was like a cloud in his eyes.

"I'll give him back his coin," he groaned.

"What are you talking about?"

"His coin, his coin," hissed Gabriel.

"Who?"

"Your Papa."

She paused for a moment. "Papa won't need his coin."

"He can have it, as long as I can keep you."

She remembered how they had teased, under Papa's willow tree. A tear rose into her eye. He was struggling to put it all together.

"But our children...."

She touched his lips gently. He was wheezing hard.

"I tried to...." His eyes rolled back with exhaustion. "I'm burning." He turned his head slightly. "Hello, Géline? Where am I?"

He had no more. It was the last of his breath. The wheezing stopped. Gabriel had stepped out from his eyes. She gathered his thin shoulders in her arms and held him close.

"Home," she whispered. "We're home."

His hair was wet on her cheek. The candle stirred. His head hung on her lap. The sun was down.

"Evangéline."

She awoke with a start. Gabriel was on the pallet beside her. It was not his voice. But it spoke her name properly, in a familiar tone. She looked around. The windows were bright with a new day. In a corner, she saw Mary walking quietly among the pallets, tending to other victims.

"Evangéline," came the soft exhortation once again.

She looked toward the door. Baptiste was standing there, his cap in both hands. She rose and went to him, unsteadily. His eyes sparkled with fond recognition, a bright blush on his face as she approached. Although he was in old tattered woollens, he stood with that same air of reverence as when he first wore the white shirt and breeches which old René had got him for his ninth New Year. Same old Baptiste! Her *petit chien*. She rubbed her face.

"Sorry to wake you," he said. "But we'll be on our way soon."

She took his hand between hers.

"What are you doing here?"

"We're going north. Four ox carts loaded for Acadie. The new governor in Halifax has made us welcome."

She gazed at him.

"How did you find me?" she said at length.

"I've been looking along the way. I remembered our first winter here. You liked the Quakers."

She drew in her breath. "You're going home?"

Baptiste nodded. "Emilie says for you to come. She's

waiting with the others at Callowhill. We're stocking up at the market."

Evangéline groped for thoughts that could make sense.

"Emilie is alive?"

"And she's cut her hair!"

"Little Emilie. So many died. And she's alive."

"I don't know how," he said, shrugging his shoulders. "But she wants you to come. Monsieur Basile sends his regards, and to say that Gabriel has done your house. But now he's looking for you among the Hurons. When he gets home, Basile will send him to Acadie."

Evangéline was fighting the storm that raged inside her.

"I don't know," she whispered.

"Don't stay here. The fever will take you. Gaston says you're to come and he's your big brother."

"He wasn't much of a brother after Papa died."

"But I can look after you."

They stood silent amidst the groans and creaking pallets. Their eyes didn't meet.

"I'd better go," he said at last.

"Why did you come today?"

Baptiste looked at her, a little confused.

"We're passing through, that's all."

"I know, Baptiste. But why today?"

"Why not today?"

A deep stillness filled the space between them. She didn't turn to look back at the pallet. *Why not today?* His hand came awkwardly to her shoulder and, for a moment, held her tightly.

"*Adieu*, Evangéline."

His eyes had never been sadder. She let go of his hand

and he headed for the stairs. She heard him walking across the gravel outside. Chickadees were chirping on the grass. As she reached the bedside again, her eyes gave in to the tears. It was a relief, as if the weeping gave her back her full breathing. She bent her mouth toward Gabriel's lips, but halted herself. On those lips was the plague. He was no longer in this life. But she was. And she could not let go of everything, to follow him to the darkness. In spite of all things, there was life. She couldn't stop now. She leaned toward the candle. With an infinitely tender breath, she bent the flame until it went out.

I have to go, Gabriel. They're waiting for me. We go like the geese. Thousands and thousands of miles. Father Félicien taught us that, remember? Almost a thousand years ago. But they always find their way back. They stretch their necks into the wind and go, safe in the hand of God.